THE WITCH'S BRAT

THE WITCH'S BRAT

by Rosemary Sutcliff

illustrated by Richard Lebenson

NEW YORK   HENRY Z. WALCK, INC.

Sutcliff, Rosemary
  The witch's brat; illus. by Richard
Lebenson.   Walck, 1970
  145p. illus.

  Biographical information: p.145
  A stirring novel of a crippled boy
in twelfth-century England.

1. Great Britain - History - Norman
period, 1066-1154 - Fiction
2. Physically handicapped - Fiction
I. Illus.   II. Title

This Main Entry catalog card may be reproduced without permission.

For Margaret, who was trained in Saint Bartholomew's Hospital, and who only likes my earlier books, because she says the later ones are too bloody.

Here is another of the earlier kind, with my love.

CONTENTS

INTRODUCTION

Augustinian canons, often called Austin canons, are something between cloistered monks and ordinary parish clergy. They belong to communities, often with a school or a hospital attached, but they live and work out in the world among ordinary people, not shut away from it.

That is how it is today, and that is how it was in the time of Rahere the King's Jongleur.

Lovel, and most of the other people in this story, are imaginary. But Rahere, the King's Jongleur who founded a great hospital, was a real person, and you can visit his tomb in the Church of Saint Bartholomew the Great, in Smithfield, London, today. His figure lies there carved in stone, in the dress of an Austin canon, and at his head and feet kneel two small figures in the same dress, reading from Latin bibles.

> For the Lord shall comfort Zion. He will comfort all her waste places, and He will make her wilderness like Eden, and her desert like the garden of the Lord; joy and gladness shall be found therein, thanksgiving and the voice of melody.

THE WITCH'S BRAT

I

"DRIVE HIM OUT!"

The boy came stumbling down between the two big outfields of the village, on his way back from taking Gyrth
the shepherd his supper. It was October, and soon Gyrth
would be bringing the sheep down from the summer pas-
ture; but at this time of year, when the rams were running with the ewes, he stayed up on the Downs with the
flock whole days and nights together. It had rained in the
early morning, and the steep rutted chalk of the driftway
was slippery, so that anybody would have to go carefully;
but the boy, Lovel, had to go more carefully than most,
because he was built crooked, with a hunched shoulder
and a twisted leg that made him walk lopsided like a bird
with a broken wing. His bony face under the thatch of
dusty dark hair was quick and eager and wanted to be
friendly; but nobody had ever bothered to notice his face;

unless perhaps it was his grandmother, and she had died a
week ago.

From the top stretch of the driftway the village was
hidden by the shoulder of the Downs, but as one rounded
the corner by the hawthorn windbreak, rusty-red now
with berries that the thrushes loved, suddenly there it was
below in the valley. The one long street with the villeins'
cottages on either side, the field strips where Osric was
sowing the winter wheat, and at the far end where the
ground rose a little, the thatched timber hall of Sir Richard d'Eresby, the Lord of the Manor, among its byres
and barns and apple trees, its bee-skeps and its great dove-
cote. And village and Knight's Hall alike were all softly
hazed over by the blue smoke of evening cooking fires
hanging low in the autumn air.

Lovel checked and stood looking down, picking out
from the rest, where it stood a little apart among the
streamside alders, the turf-roofed bothie where he had
lived with his grandmother all the eleven years since he
came into the world and his mother went out of it. With
his father, too, but his father had died last year of the
spring sickness that came often after a bad winter and
was sometimes stronger even than his grandmother's
medicine herbs.

After that, by the usual laws of the manor, his grandmother should have been turned out of the cottage to
make room for another villein and his family; but she had
been nurse and foster-mother to the old Lord's son, him

that had died when the English charged at Teuchbrai, and so she had been allowed to stay on.

Lovel dug the kale plot and looked after Garland the cow, and helped her gather her hedgerow simples and tend the little herb plot behind the cottage. And people brought her things, a hatful of apples or a new baked loaf, in payment for charming away their warts or telling them where to find their strayed cattle, for a pot of green wound-salve (there was no better in all West Sussex) or a nosegay of certain scented herbs gathered at New Moon, which, if a girl wore it tucked into the breast of her gown, would make the lad she wanted look in her direction. So what with one thing and another, she and Lovel had never gone hungry. Not too hungry, anyway.

Lovel looked away from the little humped tawny roof among the alder trees, that was home no more. He lived with Gyrth's wife and children now; Sir Richard's bailiff had arranged it, giving them the cow in payment. Gyrth's wife had welcomed the cow, but not Lovel; and she had made it painfully clear that she only gave him house-room because she had to. Well, Lovel thought, she's kind to Garland, anyway. And that was something. It seemed to him just then that there was not much kindness in the world, and he was glad that Garland should have some of it.

A late yellow butterfly hovering past caught at his attention, and he watched it dance downward and settle on a dusty stem of shepherd's purse beside the way. And for

a sort of gleam of time, he seemed to see it not only with
his eyes, but with all of himself, the delicate veining of
the yellow wings that quivered and half-closed and fanned
open again, the dark velvety nap on the butterfly's slender
body, the gray-green heart-shaped seedpods of the shepherd's purse, stirring in the stray breath of wind, sharing
with the butterfly the last warmth of the autumn sun; and
the shadow of both tangled in the hillside grass. Part of
him longed to catch the butterfly, to hold it very carefully
prisoned in his cupped hands and feel the life of it there
and the flutter of its wings against his hollowed palms, as
though in that way he could keep the small, shining
moment from escaping. He had tried that once, when he
was much younger, but the butterfly had turned broken
and dead in his hands, and he had killed the moment and
the shine and the beauty instead of keeping it, and been
left with nothing but an empty feeling of desolation in
his stomach because he could not mend the butterfly again.
His grandmother had found him with the tiny, pitiful
broken thing in his hand, and he had not told her anything, not anything at all; but she had taken his face
between her harsh, withered old hands and looked far
down into him in the queer way she had that made her
not quite like other people, and said, "So you have it too.
Throw this one away now, it's no good grieving, and not
even I can mend a broken butterfly. But one day you will
mend other things. You will be one of the menders of
this world; not the makers, nor yet the breakers, just one

of the menders." And then she had laughed and said, "It's no good bidding you to remember that. Five's too little to be remembering such things; but when the time comes, you'll know." And she had given him a piece of honeycomb in his supper bowl of barley stirabout.

It was after that that she had started taking him with her when she went to gather simples, explaining to him the uses of the different herbs.

The yellow butterfly had taken to the air again, and went dancing and zigzagging off across the outfield. The moment was over. And Lovel turned back to the village. It was still the same village that he had known all his life, but it had put on a stranger's face, and he had to take a small sharp pull at his courage before he could go on down the driftway.

There were people about in the street when he reached it, for it was almost sunset, and men were coming home from their work in the field strips or in the Lord's demesne fields, to the kale broth and brown rye bread that the women would have ready for them.

There would be kale broth and rye bread for him too, in Gyrth's cottage, but no homecoming. And as he drew nearer, he walked slower and slower still, knowing that he would get into trouble anyway for being so long away, and might as well get into a bit more while he was about it. Wulfgar the hayward had a lean cow tethered on the bit of rough ground beside his cottage, and Lovel stopped to stare at it, partly because that would put off getting back to Gyrth's cottage a few moments longer. He thought it didn't look well, and wondered if it had eaten something in the grass that was harming it. His grandmother would have known. . . . He was staring at the cow and wondering, when the hayward's wife stuck her head out of the door and shouted at him, "Get away with you! Off, or I'll call my man!"

"I wasn't doing any harm," Lovel said.

The woman's face was red-angry and at the same time oddly afraid. "No harm?" she shrilled. "No harm? Didn't you come by and stand staring at her three days since? And wasn't she fine and hearty then? Now look at her!"

"I think she's eaten something," said Lovel, scared of the woman's shrilling voice but standing his ground.

"Eaten something, say you? What's she eaten but good sweet grass? I'll tell you what's amiss with her—I'll—"

The hayward appeared in the doorway behind her, munching a crust thick with ewe-milk cheese, to see what all the noise was about; some men on their way home to supper stopped and drew closer, women and children began to appear from the nearest cottages.

"What is it, then?" somebody asked.

" 'Tis the witch's brat, staring at our cow again! Only three days since, she was well enough; and there he was a'staring and a'staring at her, and now look at her—no more nor skin and bones!"

"Happen he's put the Evil Eye on her," somebody suggested.

And others nodded their heads in agreement, "Surely."

And then somebody said, "Drive him out, the misshapen imp!"

Lovel saw their faces, more faces every moment, angry and stupid and afraid. And then everything seemed to go very small and clear and distant; and he felt as though he wasn't inside himself at all, but standing aside and watching, and understanding in a cold far-off sick sort of way exactly what was happening.

Because his grandmother had had the Wisecraft, the Old Wisdom and the Old Skills, they had come to her, all these people, when they had the toothache or a cow was sick or the butter wouldn't "come" in the churn. But because they did not understand her wisdom or her skills, they had been afraid of her too. And they had looked at Lovel himself sideways because he was her grandson and because he was crooked and for them the two things were linked together. So now that she was dead, they were letting loose on him the fear that they had felt for her.

Someone held out a hand toward him and made the Sign of the Horns with their fingers to divert ill-luck.

It was when he saw that they were afraid, that Lovel began to be really afraid, too. The faces crowded nearer. They had open mouths shouting at him to get out and take his Evil Eye with him. They were all mouths and eyes. And then a boy took up a stone from the road and threw it. It grazed his chin and drew blood; and suddenly there was a shower of stones flying round his head; and

Lovel was back inside himself again, and not thinking anymore but only terrified. And he turned and ran as best he could, stumbling on his lame leg, with the stones whistling past his ears; a small driven animal with the terror of the hunt upon him.

A few of the boys followed him to the edge of the village, and threw a parting scatter of stones and earth clods after him. One of them hit him on the shoulder and brought him down; but he struggled up again and ran on, panting and sobbing, making like a hunted wild thing for the cover of the trees; and fell at last, full-length on the woodshore where the Weeldan Forest ended in a scrub of hazel and elder and brambles at the edge of the cultivated land.

He lay quite still on his face, shuddering from head to foot, snatching at his breath, and listening, above the drumming of his heart, for any sound of the hunt behind him. But there was no sound except the brushing of a little wind through the branches, and somewhere the cry of an early hunting owl.

And presently he struggled to his feet again, aching and bruised from head to foot, and dragged himself farther in among the trees. He had never been in the forest at night before. Only the bravest of the village folk would set foot among the trees between Owl Hoot and Cock Crow, for fear of the things that lurked there. But he was not afraid, not anymore, of anything among the trees; he knew now that the forest was kinder than men. Men were the only thing one really had to be afraid of.

A hollow under the roots of an ancient slant-driven oak tree offered him shelter; and he crawled in and lay down, pressed close against the living strength of the tree, and slept.

II

WESTWARD WITH THE SUN

When the lances of the autumn sunrise slanted through the night mist among the trees, Lovel woke. He lay for a few moments wondering why he ached so much, and how he came to be there; and then he remembered, and panic began to whimper up in him. He dragged himself out of his cave of tree roots, and got to his feet again, looking around as though he expected to see his hunters come crashing through the undergrowth. He must get farther away—farther away from that dreadful village, so far that nobody would ever find him again. And then? He didn't know; he thought maybe the simplest thing would be just to lie down somewhere and die. But not yet, not until he was safe from the village.

He hadn't anything to gather up or any food to eat, so he just started walking. It was hard going in the forest, with tree roots to trip him and soft patches where old fallen trunks had turned to tinder that looked solid until one trod on them and broke through. Low-hanging branches whipped his face, brambles caught at his old russet tunic and tried to hold him back. The forest was a less friendly place today than it had been last night; but he never thought of turning back. He struggled on until the trees began to thin and it looked as though he might be coming to a clearing, perhaps another village; a village would mean men. He must go carefully. He wanted no more to do with men.

But when the big trees gave place to the usual wood-shore tangle of hazel and hawthorn and wayfaring trees, he saw in front of him not a clearing or a village, but a great slow lift of turf that swept up and up in rounded masses and bush-filled hollows, until, far above him, it made huge patient whale-backed shapes against the sky. The Downs again, but not the Downs that he knew around his old home. Those Downs were broken up into islands and great turf hills and hummocks, with the forest running everywhere between; these were a single wave-break of turf running—so far as he could see—from the sunrise to the sunset.

Born and bred in the Down country as he was, it seemed natural to him to follow the Downs now. But which way? "Always go with the sun," his grandmother had told him once, stirring some herb brew over the fire. "Against the sun, that is widdershins, that is for the Black Magic. Always with the sun." She had meant stir-

ring the brew; but her words came back to Lovel now and
seemed to have another meaning. So he went westward,
with the sun.

He had forgotten about lying down and dying; something
seemed to keep him on his feet and moving on. He lay
down when it grew dark each evening, but always
dragged himself up again when the light came back. He
lived on hedge-nuts and brambles; and once when he was
very near starving, he came close to a village and found
a hen laying abroad, and sucked the warm eggs from her
nest. But how many times he lay down, or how many
times he dragged his aching body up again, he never
knew, anymore than he knew where he was going. He
was not thinking very clearly; he only knew that he was
going with the sun.

Gradually as he went, the Downs were changing, growing broader and more shallow, with great wooded valleys
and low grazing land and river meadows breaking
through; and still he moved westward, making wide loops
to avoid villages of men who would throw stones, casting
up and down streamsides to find pack bridges or the
shallow places where the cattle crossed; but still he kept
moving westward, along the run of the Downs. If the
weather had broken he would have died, but day after
day passed quiet and almost warm like Saint Martin's
Summer. All the same, though he did not know it, he
was growing weaker, covering less distance every day.

On the last day he covered little more than a mile, and

everything around him seemed to shift and change like a dream. That evening the weather broke, and the wind rose and fine cold rain came blowing in from the west, driving him down for shelter into the valley woods. Only a narrow strip of forest before the trees fell back on the edge of cultivated land; but he did not turn back into the forest depths as he would have done a few days ago, but crept nearer and nearer to the edge of the trees, remembering vaguely the warmth of hens' eggs and hoping for another nest. And then, through the trees on the very edge of the open land, he saw the red flicker of firelight and smelled the warm companionable smell of pigs.

Not really knowing what he did, but drawn by the promise of warmth and the companionable smell, he gathered up the last of his strength, and stumbled toward the red flicker through the trees.

A dog began to bark furiously, and two lean hairy bodies came leaping toward him; and then he was on his back, held down by a dog's paws—a wolf's paws?—on his chest, and its muzzle was snarling over him, lips curled back over long white teeth; and beyond that one another, ready to fly at his throat. He heard a man's shout, and footsteps crashing through the undergrowth; the dogs were thrust aside—dogs, then, not wolves—and a man was bending over him, hands on knees.

The man said something, and it had the sound of a question, but the words could not make sense through the high white singing in his head. The man tried again, louder; but still the words could not get through. Lovel crouched on the ground and shook his head. The world had begun going round and round. He heard the man curse, and felt himself picked up in a pair of very strong arms; and had just time to notice that the man had the same warm thick smell of pigs, before the whirling and singing in his head turned into a kind of spinning funnel, and he was sucked down into it, faster and faster into the dark.

The next thing he knew was the warm red flame-flicker of the fire and the smell of pigs all around him. He lay still, blinking at the flames, while gradually other things began to take shape—the swineherd himself squatting on his heels and tending something in a pannikin among the hot fringes of the fire; the dogs, no longer

looking at all like wolves, lying one on either side of him with their long frilled tongues hanging out of their mouths, and beyond them among the tree trunks the humped dark shapes of sleeping pigs.

He moved a little, carefully, so as not to set the world spinning again, and the man looked around. "Better, eh?"

Lovel nodded. He was not afraid of this man.

"Hungry, too, I daresay."

Lovel thought about this doubtfully for a few moments, then nodded again.

The swineherd looked at him more closely. "Not dumb are you, as well as all the rest?"

Lovel just stopped himself from shaking his head. "No —I—I—" His tongue felt heavy as though it were made of wood. "Not dumb."

"On the run, are you?" the man said shrewdly after a few moments.

"No, I—got lost."

The swineherd ignored this. "Been on the run some time by the looks of you. 'Tisn't no good, you know, better go back to your manor and take your punishment, whatever it is."

"No!" Lovel dragged himself into a sitting position, the world slipping and swimming about him. "And you can't make me; I won't tell you where it is!"

"Well now, we'll see about that later," said the swineherd, and took the pannikin off the fire and poured some of the thick lumpy stirabout into a wooden bowl and pushed it at Lovel. "Get that inside you, and you can sleep here by the fire tonight anyways."

Lovel supped the warm stirabout that tasted, as everything smelled in these parts, of pigs; and lay down again under the old bit of sack that the swineherd spread over him.

At first he slept deep and dark, but as the night wore on he began to toss and turn and wake up more and more often, sometimes very hot and sometimes shivering with cold, and sometimes both together. And when morning came and pigs and dogs and swineherd roused all together, the queer feeling that everything was a dream had come back more strongly than ever so that Lovel was not sure if he were really there at all.

The swineherd was most put out. "Here's a fine tangle!" he grumbled. "I was going to let you go—and a fool I'd have been, I know—and told anyone as asked that I hadn't seen nobody pass this way; but you're in no state to go a'roaming round the forest dropping dead all over the place, and that's flat."

Lovel said nothing. It was hard to think straight, in his dream, let alone argue.

"Well, there's nowt for it but I'll have to get you back to the Abbey for the Holy Fathers to look after," said the swineherd. "And the sooner the better." He made sure that the fire was out, and spoke to the dogs as though they were Christians, bidding them look after the swine, who had already scattered and begun their day-long snuffing and rooting after acorns, and keep them from straying before he got back, for if he found one missing he'd have the tails off them. Then he turned back to Lovel, "Come on, up with you now—can you walk?"

Lovel could, but only just, because the forest floor with its soft dark covering of leaf-mold felt as though it was made of mist under his feet.

"Hold up, Hobgoblin," said the swineherd and grabbed him by the arm, not unkindly.

Stumbling along with the swineherd's grip crushing his arm, Lovel was vaguely aware that they had left the trees and then that they were following a driftway like the one that led between the outfields of his old village, but not so steep, and made of mud instead of wet chalk. But almost at once his legs folded under him and he stumbled and fell; and the swineherd grunted like one of his own pigs, and picked him up. "Ah well, 'twill be quicker to carry you in the long run, I reckon, and you don't weight no more than a t'Anthony's piglet."

Lovel shut his eyes, somehow things were better with his eyes shut, now that he didn't have to look where he was going; and for a while there was nothing but swimming darkness and the jog-jog-jog of being carried. When he opened his eyes again, the swineherd was carrying him in through a gateway with an arched roof, and inside it there were tall buildings—Lovel had never seen such tall buildings, especially a tower in their midst that soared up and up as though to take the sky on its strong shoul-

ders. A bell rang out from the tall tower, and the bright
echoes of it swooped and darted around inside his head
like swallows. And then there were men in black habits,
and one of them, with a bleak face, was asking him questions. The man's voice was dry and brittle like dead sticks,
but Lovel could not understand what he said for the bell-
notes swooping around in his head; and at last the man
said something impatiently to another and went away.

And then there were roof beams between him and sky,
and lying down, and being covered by a rug, and some
kind of bitter broth in a bowl. And then there was nothing but the dream for a long time.

III

NEW MINSTER

One morning, Lovel woke up with his head feeling quite
clear again, though he was so weak that he could hardly
turn it on the rustling straw-filled pillow, to look about
him and see where he was.

He was in a long narrow room like a hall, with lime-
washed walls and high windows, and more pallet beds like
the one he lay on ranged down the length of it; but all
the others were empty. And opening from the long room,
halfway down, was a little chapel with candles glimmering in the morning light, before an altar and the green
and crimson and dim-gold picture of a saint.

A man in the black habit of a Benedictine monk came
out from the little glowing chapel and walked toward
him. Not the bleak-faced man he had seen before, but a

much younger one who seemed to have come often into his dream; small and plump, and pink as a campion, with a hopeful expression, and a fringe of carrot-red curls around his head.

He stooped over Lovel, and felt his forehead, and nodded. "Ah now, this is better! Much better! This is much, much, *much* better!" he said in a quick chirping voice. "No fever at all. God's greeting to you, my child, now that you are back with us again."

But Lovel was bewildered by his strange surroundings and still confused from the long tangled days and nights of his dream, and out of all this, he caught at only one word, because it was a word that terrified him. "Back? Please no! Don't send me back! I won't go back—I *can't*!" He tried to sit up, but he was too weak, and fell onto the pillow again.

"No one is sending you back," said the little plump kindly monk. "No, no, no, of course not! Now lie still, and you shall have some gruel, and then you will sleep, and by God's Grace you will wake up quite strong again. Yes, yes, strong enough to push houses over."

And the sudden fear that had leaped up in Lovel sank down again and crept away to where it came from. He was almost asleep when the little monk came back with the gruel; but it smelled so good, hot and milky and as though there was honey in it, that suddenly the soft warm water came into his mouth and he knew that he was hungry. He was just thinking about dragging his eyes open and waking up, when he realized that somebody else was standing at the foot of the bed and looking at him.

He had learned that he need not be afraid of the swineherd, nor of the little monk. But of all other men and women and children he was still very much afraid. They were the Throwers of Stones, the Hunt on his trail. He was wide awake on the instant. But he lay quite still, and kept his eyes shut, because he couldn't escape, and so shamming sleep seemed the best thing to do.

"Well now, if he isn't asleep again!" chirped the little monk softly. "Poor child, poor child . . . I daresay sleep will do him even more good than gruel at this stage."

The other man spoke consideringly, and at once Lovel knew the dry brittle voice. "It was convenient that he talked so freely in his fever. Otherwise if he is as frightened as you say, he would probably have refused to tell us where he came from at all, and I imagine we should have had some difficulty in tracing his manor."

Under the blanket and in the dark behind his closed eyes, Lovel stopped breathing. He was not just wary and shamming sleep now, he was cold with terror, frozen like some small defenseless animal when the shadow of the hawk hangs overhead. If they knew where he came from, they could send him back. He was a villein, bound to the land, not even free to run away—and he was trapped!

Then his own little fat monk said, "Brother Eustace, you are *sure* there is no question of sending him back?"

"My dear Brother Peter." The other man sounded more

brittle than ever with impatience. "I had it from the Father Abbot himself. Sir Richard does not want him back —he's as good as useless, after all, and the rest of the manor villeins it seems are convinced he has the Evil Eye, so he would really be more trouble than he's worth. He confides the boy into our hands." Then with a burst of irritation, "It is truly wonderful how the world looks on every house of God as a convenient cupboard in which to stow their lame and witless safely out of the way."

"Don't! Please don't, Brother Eustace! I cannot—I really cannot bear to hear you pretending to be so heartless—"

Brother Eustace sighed. "For an infirmarer, as for any physician, there are two ways. One is to bleed a little of your own life away with every sick soul who passes through your hands—that will be your way, when you are Infirmarer after me. The other is to do all that may be done for the sick; but stand well back while doing it. That

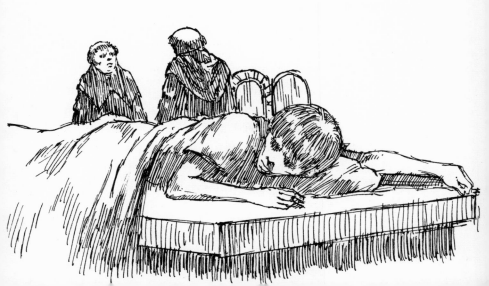

way you don't break your heart. That is my way, Brother
Peter, and I really think the sick recover just as well and
as often for me as they do for you." His voice sounded
as though he was moving away. "It is no use leaving that
gruel, it will only get cold. Bring him some more later."

"Gruel—yes, yes of course; you're perfectly right,"
Brother Peter said absently. "But as to the rest—I don't
believe God would agree with you. I know you think I'm
very foolish but I really don't—"

Lovel lay still and listened to the scuff of their sandals
and Brother Peter's unhappy chirps of protest dying away
into the distance.

He was no longer afraid, only filled with a cold gray
misery. A desolation that seemed to fill all the world and
leave nothing over.

And he was still very hungry, and wanted the gruel
with honey in it that they had taken away.

So Lovel stayed on at the minster.

It was the great minster that had once had its home
within the walls of the royal city of Winchester; until the
Father Abbot and the monks and something called the
Foundation, which he learned was really the minster
much more than the old monastery buildings and the old
church were, had moved a mile outside the city, to the
fine new buildings that were not quite finished even yet.
People called it the New Minster—but then they always
had, even when it was still inside the city walls. So as

Brother Peter said when he explained all this to Lovel, there was nothing new in *that*.

The life of the place folded itself around him, until sometimes as the winter went by, it was hard to believe he had ever known any other life. Only that he still dreamed sometimes at night of faces that were all eyes and open mouths, crowding in on him, and stones whistling round his ears.

He slept in the long garret above the storerooms, where the rest of the monastery's inside servants slept; and every morning he went with them and the farm people to the Mass that was held especially for them between the service of Prime and the monks' breakfast. It was never decided whether he was one of the Abbot's servants, or belonged to the bakehouse or the stables, the garden, the brewhouse or the kitchen. Nothing about him was ever quite decided, so he had no particular place of his own in the life of the minster. But he got used to it, and used to answering shouts from all the rest. "Hi, you! Come and turn the spit!" "Carry out the pig-swill, Humpy." "Go and find that good-for-nothing Jehan and tell him I want him!"

For the most part, his world was the great outer court, around which were ranged the monastery workshops and storehouses, stables and kitchens, and guest-lodgings. The monastery had many guests, for the road from London that passed the gatehouse was always busy with people coming and going to Winchester, especially when the King held court there, or to the great seaport town of

Southampton a dozen miles beyond. Merchants and knights, seamen and beggars, strolling ballad-sellers, pilgrims on their way to Rome or back.

The builders were still at work there too, enlarging the stables; and on saints' days the people from all around flocked in to church. And often people would come—Saxons for the most part, but sometimes one speaking the Norman French that all men spoke in court and castle, to visit the minster's chief-most treasure, the tomb before the High Altar where, under a plain slab of Purbeck stone carved with a cross and the two words *Alfredus Rex,* King Alfred lay with his battles all behind him.

So what with one thing and another, the hustle and bustle in the outer court went on all the daylight hours, till sometimes Lovel's head fairly spun with it.

But beyond the high doors into the cloisters, where he seldom went, it was so quiet that the scuff of a monk's sandaled feet sounded like an interruption, and the Brethren passed each other in silence, their hands hidden in their sleeves and their eyes cast down. Only from the North Cloister would come the drone of the novices repeating their lessons.

To Lovel, going through that door from the outer court was like going from one world into another. But high over both worlds, the bell would ring for Matins or Lauds, Vespers or Prime; the round bronze sound of it like a stone dropped into a pool, the widening ripples humming and thrumming away till they were lost in the silence again; and the plainsong would echo to and fro in the deep Gregorian chant, among the high empty spaces of the minster church that had doors opening into both worlds because it belonged to both.

One evening just after Candlemas, when the King and his Court were at Winchester, a great gale blew up, driving the stinging sleet before it. In the firelit monastery kitchen one of the cooks, pounding fennel in a mortar to flavor the next day's fish, said, "Heaven have pity on any traveler abroad tonight!" And the very moment after he had said it, there was a lull in the booming wind, and they all heard the sound of horses' hooves ringing hollow under the arch of the gatehouse. Then the wind swooped back, smothering all sounds from outside.

The servants looked at each other in the red light of fire and torches. "Ours, or the Hospitaler's?" somebody said; for the pilgrims and poorest travelers were lodged in the big bare hospice next to the gatehouse, where Brother Dominic the Hospitaler looked after them, while the knights and merchants were housed in the guest chambers and looked after by the Abbot's servants; and the great lords were entertained by the Abbot himself, in his own lodging.

A little later the Abbot's Steward came through the door from the lodging, and looked around at the cooks and scullions and table servers, all busily at work under the Master Cook's watchful eye. "Take lights, and wood for a fire up to the Nazareth Chamber; it is the least drafty

of the guest quarters in this wind; food also when it is
ready—the best we can provide. The storm has blown us a
guest."

When he had gone, the Master Cook said, "And not one
his High and Mightiness relishes much, by the look on
his face. Sour as perjuice!" He looked around to see who
was least busy at the moment, and his eye fell on Lovel,
who had just come in from the brewhouse with the big
jug of ale he had been sent to fetch and was waiting to
be told what to do next.

"Hi, you! Humpy, go and fetch some wood and take it
up to the Nazareth Chamber; and mind you take dry
logs, not ones from the pile that's still green, as you did
last time!"

Lovel ducked out again into the wild night, where the
wind swooped across the great courtyard like a live thing.
It was dusk already, and the high tower of the minster
church had lost itself in the driving sleet. A riding horse
and an unloaded baggage pony were being led into the
stable as he made for the woodstore; and in the light of
the shielded stable lantern he saw that the horse was a
good one, red as a chestnut, and moving like a courser,
the kind, he had learned since he came to the minster,
that a knight rode when traveling.

The wide thatched eaves of the woodstore, and the
wattle work sheathing half its open side kept out most
of the sleet, and he found the stack of dry logs, and
spread the big sacking carry-cloth on the ground and

dumped as many logs onto it as he could possibly carry,
then gathered up the ends and started back with them.

Lugging the heavy bundle of logs across the forecourt,
he saw the torchlight in the window of the Nazareth
Chamber. The Nazareth Chamber and the Abbot's Lodging had real glass in the windows, like the church only
not colored; so the shutters did not have to be closed to
keep the wind out. Lovel wondered who was in there—a
rich merchant with embroidered silks from Byzantium?
a knight in rain-rusted mail, homing from a war in
foreign parts?

In the entrance to the Guest Lodging, Jehan, the oldest
and largest of the scullions, met him and grabbed the
bundle of logs. "Those won't be enough, you mooncalf!
Go and get some more."

Lovel went back across the courtyard. In the lantern-lit
stable the horse was being rubbed down while the baggage
pony stood waiting his turn; and he checked on his way
to the woodstore and stood looking in. Harding, the old
man-at-arms who saw to the monastery's horses, was a
friend of his, and so was Valiant, his big mongrel dog.
Valiant came padding across now to poke a welcoming
muzzle into Lovel's hand, and Harding looked around
from his task and grinned. "He's a beauty, isn't he?"

Lovel nodded. He saw the harness that had just been
taken off and hung up over the manger; not the harness of
a knight's horse, surely, for it was hung with little bells.
"Who is it?" he asked.

"Our guest? Why, it's Rahere."

"Rahere?"

"Oh o'course, you wouldn't know him; he's not been here-along since well before your time. Rahere, the King's Jongleur. Well they do say he's more of a minstrel, really; that's higher ranking, like. And there's some says he's just a natural-born fool with a gift for making the King laugh. But if you was to ask me, he has too fine a taste in horse flesh to be any kind of fool."

And he returned to hissing through his teeth and rubbing away at the damp gleaming chestnut flanks with his whisp of hay.

Lovel went and got the logs; as many as he could carry piled up under his chin. Jehan still had the carry-cloth, so that would have to do. Then he set out once more for the lit window of the Nazareth Chamber.

Again Jehan met him in the doorway. "What d'you think you're up to? You've been all night, Humpy!" And then without waiting for an answer, "All right, give me the logs and get back to the kitchen."

Lovel started to protest. He had had all the work of fetching the wood, and now he was to be robbed of his sight of the King's Jongleur. "The King's Jongleur"—the words were singing themselves over in his head. They never let him see or do anything interesting! But Jehan had already grabbed the logs from him and slammed the heavy door in his face.

Standing there in the dark and the sleet, face to face

with the blank uncaring door timbers, a sudden fire of
revolt rose in Lovel's chest, and all at once it mattered more
than anything else in the world that he should see this
Rahere, this King's Jongleur. In some queer way that he
did not understand and certainly had no time to think
out, it was as though if he did not, he would be accept-
ing doors slammed in his face all the rest of his life.

He had enough sense left to know that if he simply
pushed the door open again and went in, he would only
run slap into Jehan and get his head half knocked off and
be kicked outside again before he got so much as a
glimpse of this Rahere. So he tried the lighted window; but
the deep embrasure was too high above his head, and
he could find no way of pulling himself up to it. It
would have to be the door—but not until Jehan had gone.
He slipped into the angle behind a buttress, and squatted
down. It was not a very good hiding place, but it was
almost full-dark now, and anyone passing would be in a
hurry and have his head tucked well down against the
sleet.

It was bitterly cold and he began to shiver from head
to foot, but luckily he had not long to wait before the
door opened and shut again, and Jehan came out, jingling
coins in his hand, and disappeared into the kitchen buildings. Now! If he was going to do it at all he must do it
now, before other people came with water for the guest
to wash his hands or linen for the table. Any moment
they might come! Lovel stumbled out from his hiding

place to the Guest Lodging door; he opened it and slipped inside, and managed to get it shut again without letting it bang in the wind.

After the storm outside it seemed very warm and still and quiet. A torch burning in a wall sconce showed him three or four steps on his right leading down to a kind of undercroft; and on his left, several more leading up into a narrow slipway. And just where the slipway lost itself in darkness, the door of the Nazareth Chamber stood ajar, letting out a broad stripe of torchlight to paint itself on the opposite wall. Letting out also the chattering and whistling and soft fluting notes of a starling. Rahere must have a tame bird in there; and as Lovel checked, looking and listening, a long-legged fantastic shadow flickered across the torchlight on the wall, and was gone.

Lovel was suddenly frightened. It all seemed like the beginning of a dream; and you never could tell with dreams. But he never thought of turning back. He crept up the steps and reached the door without a sound, and poked his head far enough around it to squint into the room with one eye.

He could see the end of a bed hung with dark colored stuff; a wet, fur-lined cloak flung across it, and a cap with a battered bunch of gamecock's feathers held by a jeweled clasp. Edging in a little farther he saw an unstrapped pack spilling a pair of shoes with fashionably curled toes and sundry other garments on the floor. And a pair of sleet-sodden riding boots standing beside the central hearth.

The starling was still whistling, but it and the King's Jongleur were both hidden from him by the edge of the door. He pushed it open a little farther, and then just the breadth of a thumbnail farther still.

The King's Jongleur stood in the window embrasure, looking out into the stormy dark where there could not possibly be anything to see but the black-and-trickling-silver beyond the reflected torches, and whistling like a starling under the eaves.

IV

THE KING'S JONGLEUR

Rahere's back was long and lanky, and starling-dark
from head to toe. Dark hair made darker still with wet at
the ends; full-sleeved tunic of some wonderful black stuff
starling-freckled here and there with dim gold, and
hitched up short through his belt for riding. Long bony
legs in close-fitting black hose. Only where the wide
sleeves fell back, the tight sleeves of his under-tunic
showed a wonderful deep blazing green.

Lovel thought that it was the most beautiful color
he had ever seen. The perfect color for the King's
Jongleur . . .

The man in the window stopped whistling and said
without moving, "Come in then, Brother."

For an instant, Lovel froze. But the voice had not been

angry, only quietly amused. And he took a deep breath and went in.

"And pray you shut the door behind you. There is a draft in this place to split a man down the center as neatly as a pickled herring."

Lovel timidly closed the door and stood with his back to it, as Rahere turned from the window. He had a long blue-shadowed chin, clean-shaven like a monk's, and his eyes in the darkness of his face were the grayest and brightest that Lovel had ever seen. He said in the same amused tone, "Next time you want to spy on anyone, remember that a window with glass in it makes a fine mirror after dark when the torches are lit."

"I wasn't spying on you," Lovel said. "Jehan took the logs I brought for the fire and bade me get back to the kitchen, and I wanted—they said you were the King's Jongleur—"

"And so never having seen a King's Jongleur, or a unicorn, or an Ethiopian with phoenix feathers in his hair, you wished to see me. And they were mistaken—oh most woefully mistaken. I am the King's nothing. I spend much of my time about the court; I do my best for him, as it were, but not even I could stand Our Henry *all* the time."

Lovel gazed with his mouth open in awed delight at this mad and magnificent man with the monk's face and the cool mocking voice and long fantastic legs like a cranefly, who spoke English but in such splendid and far-off words that much of it was as far beyond his reach

as the Norman-French spoken by most of the knights and
wealthy travelers who passed that way, and by some of
the Brethren among themselves. And who called the King
of England "Our Henry" and could not stand him all the
time, just as though he were an ordinary human being.

Suddenly Rahere smiled. "Ah well, King's Jongleur or
no, you see me standing here before you. And fair is only
fair. Come farther into the light so that I may see you
also, small Brother."

Lovel hesitated an instant. But fair was only fair. He
took the deep breath he always took before anything difficult, and limped forward, holding himself as straight as
he could. And all the way the pale bright eyes of Rahere
watched him.

"So, that is greatly better," Rahere said. "I've a liking
for seeing the faces of the people I talk to—also for knowing their names. What do they call you?"

"Humpy, most times," Lovel said.

Rahere sat himself down in the carved chair by the
hearth, and dangled one long black leg over the arm.
There was a hole in the toe of his hose. "What pitiful
lack of invention," he said. "And do you mind?"

Lovel nodded.

"Remember that rather more than half the men in the
world are fools," said Rahere. "But remember also that
they cannot help it. And don't let it make you proud;
there's always the chance that we are the most foolish
of them all; I because I spend my time thinking of witty

things to say and songs to sing to amuse a fool in a
crown and his fool barons—" he fixed Lovel with an
anguished gaze. "Not even witty. Do you know that
when I pretend to fall over my own feet, or pull the
cushion away from under one of them as he sits down,
the rest *laugh?* You because you mind being called
Humpy . . . What is your real name?"

"Lovel."

"And you are one of the Abbot's servants, Lovel?"

Lovel was silent a moment, not quite sure how to
answer; then he said, "Not really. I'm not really anything;
I just fetch and carry and do the odd jobs nobody else
wants to do." He was not complaining, just trying to tell
the truth. "I'm not much use for anything else, you see,"
he added by way of explanation.

"Did someone tell you that?" Rahere said.

Lovel stood and rubbed one foot over the other, remembering the morning when he had woken from his
dream and heard Brother Peter and Brother Eustace talking. "They thought I was still asleep," he said.

"And they were mistaken." The King's Jongleur sat
and looked at him consideringly, with his head a little on
one side. Then he said, "I have the oddest feeling that
they were mistaken about the other thing, too."

Footsteps came up the shallow stair, the door opened,
and the Steward appeared on the threshold, backed by
servants carrying linen and silver, warm water and towels.
He saw Lovel and let out a squawk like an outraged hen,

"You! And what do you suppose you are doing here? Away with you back to the kitchen where you belong! Master Rahere, I do crave your pardon that this wretched boy has troubled you."

Lovel, with all the brightness falling around him like withered leaves, turned toward the door. But Rahere's voice pulled him up short. "Wait, Lovel," and as the boy hesitated, he withdrew that long black leg from over the arm of the chair, wagged his big toe at the Steward through the hole in his stocking as another man might wag a reproving finger, and sat up. "I saw the brat from the window and called him in, having a mind for someone to talk to."

"If you wished for converse, I am sure that one of the Holy Fathers—" began the Steward.

"Oh I didn't," sighed Rahere, "just for someone to talk to. You know what a creature of whim I am. For instance, I have a new whim opened within me—pop! Like a gorsepod—at this moment, that the brat shall stay and serve me at table, while you, after you have brought me some food and wine to eat off that fine white linen and drink out of that fine silver cup, shall go quietly back to your own place and spend your time in pious contemplation."

"But—but, Master Rahere, the boy knows nothing of such matters—"

"Then I will give him his first lesson," said Rahere.

So Lovel stayed; and very gravely and carefully served

Rahere at table, doing strange and complicated things with dishes and saltcellars and clean linen napkins exactly as the King's Jongleur bade him. And all the whole he concentrated on not spilling anything, he was puzzling at the back of his mind over the surprising fact that Rahere had called him "the brat" and it hadn't brought the sound of stones whistling round his ears. He hadn't minded at all. Perhaps it did not matter what names people called you by, only what they meant behind them.

When the meal was over, Rahere leaned back in the carved chair, stretching his arms above his head, and smiled at him out of the depth of that half-haunted face of his. "If I were the King in his palace, I might have had a richer supper, but I could not be wishing for a better page to serve before me at table."

Lovel said eagerly, "I wish you *were* the King!" and then flushed scarlet, because the words were out of his mouth before he knew it; and he had only just stopped himself in time from saying, "And I wish I *were* your page!"

"So do not I," said Rahere, and laughed.

And all the eagerness went out of Lovel like a pinched out candle; and he thought, No, and you'd not want a page the likes of me, if you were. It was only a kind of joke. But this time he did not say any of it aloud.

But Rahere put out his hands that were big and bony like the rest of him, and touched the extreme tip of a long forefinger down onto each of Lovel's shoulders, the

hunched one and the good one, so that for the moment there did not feel to be any difference between them. "Do you know, Brat, I nearly pushed on to join the King in Winchester tonight, in spite of the storm; only Bayard always shakes his ears when they are wet—flip, flap, flip, flap—the most irritating habit; and when I saw the minster gatehouse looming up, I knew that I could not endure another mile of it; so in I turned to claim shelter—and caught you peering at me through the door-chink yonder. A fine thing is chance, small Brother Lovel. . . . If I were to come back and whistle you out of here one day, would you come?"

Lovel tried to speak, but he could not. He had let out words that he hadn't meant to, and now that he wanted most desperately to speak, he couldn't find the words at all. He nodded and nodded, deeply and vehemently, hoping that Rahere would understand.

And then high in the stormy dark, the great bell in the minster tower began to ring for Compline; and Rahere got up and reached for his still damp boots. And the shining hour was over.

Next morning as he knelt with the other monastery servants at Mass in the great church, Lovel heard through the after-storm quiet and the droning voice of Brother Barnabas, the clatter of horses' hooves under the gate arch, and then trippling away, fainter and fainter down the road.

He had hoped against hope for another sight of Rahere, even from a distance. But Rahere was gone, and there was only emptiness where he had been. Lovel told himself firmly and sensibly that Rahere had come before, and one day he would come again. But all he knew just now was that Rahere was gone, and had maybe forgotten already what he had said last night about whistling for him.

His face was sore where Jehan had cuffed him to teach him not to get ideas above himself, and his knee had begun to ache, as it did when he knelt on it too long. He shifted, trying to find an easier position, and so caught a glimpse between the two men in front of him of the High Altar, glimmering, colored and gold in the shadows. He could not see the big stone slab in the pavement before it, but whenever he saw the High Altar he always thought of it there, with the carved cross and the words that Brother Anselm the Precentor, had once spelled out for him: *Alfredus Rex.*

Brother Godwyne, the oldest of all the monks of New Minster, who loved quoting the sayings of King Alfred to anybody who would listen, had told him once a saying of the King's that he hadn't even remembered two minutes later; but it came back to him now.

If thou hast a sorrow, tell it to thy saddlebow, and ride on, singing.

King Alfred must have known something about feeling cold and desolate inside, Lovel thought, before he could make a saying like that. And suddenly he felt very companionable toward the Saxon King sleeping under his stone.

Lovel hadn't got a saddlebow and he couldn't sing in tune. But he stuck out his tongue and caught the one salt-tasting tear that was trickling down his nose; and when Mass was over, went to chop up kindling for the bakehouse.

V

VALIANT

The next important thing that happened to Lovel was that he learned to read.

Brother Anselm the Precentor, who had charge of all the books in the monastery library as well as all the music in the church, found him one day looking at a book on physic herbs which had been left open in one of the library stalls, when he was supposed to be sweeping the floor; and asked him if he knew the herb drawn on that page.

"Comfrey," Lovel said. "It is good for green wounds, and for knitting broken bones."

"And who told you that?"

"My Grannie. She was very wise in healing herbs. . . . It is wonderful, you can see that it is comfrey just by looking at the picture. But does it say, down here where these words are written, that it is a wound herb?"

Brother Anselm looked at him a moment out of old
tired blue eyes that must have been the color of speedwell
before they faded. "Would you like to know all that it
says?"

Lovel nodded, suddenly too shy to say how much he
would like it. And the Precentor read to him what it said;
and then turned the other pages and showed him other
pictures, all most beautifully and lovingly drawn in
brown-black ink on creamy parchment by a monk who
had died long before the New Minster moved outside the
walls of Winchester. And some of them Lovel knew,
because they had grown in his Grannie's herb plot and
he had helped her tend them; and some were the wild-
growing simples she had brought back in her rush basket
from the woods and the Downs. And some were strangers
to him; but when he asked Brother Anselm to read him
what their words said, the old man said that if he wanted
to know what the words meant, he must learn to read
them for himself, and that he, Brother Anselm, would
teach him.

They were hard at it when Brother Eustace the Infirmarer came to put back on its shelf the book that he
had left open when he was called away to a sick monk.

Brother Anselm said, "Brother Eustace, do you think
that Brother John could do with help in the physic
garden?"

"Why?" said Brother Eustace without much interest.
And then his voice became even sharper and more brittle

than usual. "You have not been letting the boy touch that book? His hands are filthy."

Brother Anselm said very gently, "Dear Brother Eustace, the sick of this monastery are your concern; the books are mine. How many years have you been with us, Lovel?"

"More than two years, Father."

"So long? For two years we have been blind and foolish, Brother Eustace, we have made no use of this boy's special skills. We have not even troubled to find out that he had any."

"And has he?" Brother Eustace raised his brows.

"He knows nearly as much about the growing of physic herbs as Brother John himself, and he knows your own cure for the colic, and—" a gentle amusement flickered in the Precentor's voice— "some that I greatly doubt if you have ever used at all."

"That, I can well believe," the Infirmarer said.

But the Precentor was not to be turned aside from his idea, even by Brother John who was small and peppery and not at all sure that he wanted a new assistant pulling up his most cherished herbs for weeds. And within a few days, Lovel had ceased to be at everybody's beck and call, and became Brother John's helper in the physic garden, with a place of his own in the life of the monastery at last.

Eight hundred years ago, most plants counted as herbs and had their uses of one kind or another, and so the physic garden was a garden of flowers, and beautiful accordingly, though the flowers were not grown for beauty. Tall speckle-throated foxgloves stood in the shade of an old elder tree; periwinkle and herb Robert for cleansing wounds shared a bed with the white opium poppy brought back to England by the first Crusaders. Rosemary was there for headaches, and scabius and blue cranesbill; the white starred garlic; and celandines for sore eyes and camomile to bring quiet sleep; and the white or purple comfrey that helps broken bones to knit.

Lovel was happy working there, away from the rush and bustle of the kitchens and the outer court. He had time to go on learning to read; and life was much more peaceful, except, just occasionally—like the time he brought in and planted a root of yarrow, which his grandmother had always said was a better wound-wort even than dittany. Brother John said that yarrow belonged to the Devil, and that it was easy to see what Lovel's grandmother had been; and pulled up the root and threw it at his head. That night Lovel dreamed, as he had not done for a long time, of the faces that were all eyes and mouths, and the stones whistling round his ears.

But after a while, he and Brother John began to understand each other well enough. And so he went on working most of his time in the physic garden, and learning about the herbs that he tended from the great book in the library. And presently, little fat Brother Peter, and even Brother Eustace, the Father Infirmarer himself, began to call him into the infirmary stillroom to do the jobs that used up time without skill, and yet could not be left to anybody

who did not know what they were doing; chopping up
roots, pounding leaves in a mortar, watching strange
mixtures boil and taking them off the fire at the right
moment. There was always plenty of such work to do, for
Brother Eustace doctored not only the Brethren and the
monastery servants, but folk from all the surrounding
country.

And all the while, though he was not properly aware
of it, the Old Wisdom and the Old Skills that were in him
from his grandmother were waking more and more; the
Green-Fingers that could wax a plant to flourish and give
its best; the queer power of the hands on sick or hurt
bodies.

About a year after he went to work in the physic garden,
Lovel had his first patient.

He was hoeing weeds by himself, because Brother John,
with the rest of the monks, was at Vespers. Faintly,
through the thick walls of the church, he could hear their
chanting voices as he worked. From the outer court
came the clip-clop of horses' hooves and the rattle of cart-
wheels. That would be the first load of hay for the great
lofts over the stables—the May cut that smells the sweetest
and gives the best fodder. The sunlit, long-shadowed
peace of the early summer evening was scattered by a
shower of excited barks, and Lovel grinned to himself as
he hoed carefully around the roots of a rosemary bush.
Valiant was after the stable cat again! But almost in the

same instant the barking changed to an agonized yelping, and there was a shout and flurry of voices. Lovel dropped the hoe and headed at a limping run for the little door in the high wall, almost hidden by a buttress of the church, dragged it open and stumbled out into the great forecourt.

The haycart stood in the middle of the open space, with the horse backing and fidgeting uneasily in the shafts; a little group of men were gathered beside it, and in their midst, Valiant, yelping and yelping in pain and bewilderment was trying to struggle up onto three legs.

Harding had come running from the stables, and people were talking all at once, "Ran right under wheels!" "Always did say he'd chase that cat once too often."

And the loudest voice of all was Jehan's, saying, "It's broken. Best knock him on the head and be done with it."

Lovel saw the look on their faces—the look on Harding's face above all—and shouted, "No! Wait!" And next moment he was in the midst of the group, pushing his way through to where Valiant, quiet now, crouched on three legs with his head distressfully down, and his right foreleg half-tucked up at a queer unnatural angle. "Hold him for me, Harding," he said, and got down awkwardly onto his sound knee and held out a reassuring hand, "Easy, boy. Easy, Valiant, let me look."

The old man-at-arms squatted down without a word and drew the dog against his knees, and Lovel fondled the great drooping head a moment, then drew his hand

down over neck and shoulder to the injured foreleg. The
bystanders glanced at each other, grinning, or shrugged,
or looked on with surprised interest at the way Humpy
had taken command of the situation, just as though he
were one of the Brothers, with the right to order them
about.

"Look out, he'll bite," somebody said.

"He won't bite me. He's got too much sense, and he
knows I'm trying to help him." Lovel's hands were on
the place now; he could feel the break in the bone. Valiant

was shuddering from nose to tail, but he made no sound, and certainly no attempt to snap. Lovel went on feeling very carefully and gently at the broken bone, and talking reassuringly to Valiant all the time. He seemed to be seeing with his hands as well as feeling; it was all very odd. After a few moments he looked up at Harding, "It's a clean break. If we could get the ends to stay together and keep it straight long enough, it ought to mend."

The weather-beaten face of the old man-at-arms was wretched, and torn with doubt. "Can we do that? I'd not want the old lad to suffer, and all to no good in the end."

Lovel was silent a moment. He had to decide, with the dog's beautiful amber brown eyes on his face, and warm wet tongue suddenly curling out to lick his hand, whether he could really make the broken leg mend properly; or whether it would be kinder if Harding were to use his knife now, and make it all over for Valiant without any more pain. "I think so," he said at last. "I'm sure it's worth trying, even if it hurts him quite a lot. Please Harding, let me try."

Though he did not yet know it himself, there was a strange new authority in him, that had come the moment he touched the injured dog; the authority of someone doing his own job and knowing exactly what he is doing.

Harding looked down at his dog and then up again at the boy, and nodded. "Tell me what you'd have me do."

"Go on holding him like that so that he can't move

about," Lovel said; and then to the knot of bystanders, "I'll need some straight sticks, and rags—plenty of rags, torn into strips." And the surprising new authority was in his voice, too.

Somebody laughed, and said, "Hark to the Father Infirmarer!" But the sticks and a handful of rags were brought all the same. He chose the three best bits of wood for his purpose, thin but strong, and cut them to the length he wanted with somebody's knife. Then while Harding supported the broken foreleg, he began to bind them on with the strips of rag so that they held the break splinted and secure. He had to be very careful of the tension, knowing that if he made the binding too tight, Valiant's paw would die because the life could not get through to it; and if he made it too loose, the break would not be held rigid enough and the bone would not knit together. He was concentrating so hard, frowning and biting his tongue, that he lost all awareness of the little group standing around, and did not even notice that when Vespers ended, two or three of the Brothers came out from the great West Door of the church, to see what the disturbance had been about, and that one of them remained behind for a short while, watching him, after the others had gone back into the cloisters.

When the last knot was tied, Lovel sat back on his heel and thrust the hair out of his eyes, and looked about him at the outside world that he had just remembered.

He said, "I think that'll hold, so long as we can keep

him from biting at the rags. If I go now I can maybe get word with the Father Infirmarer before he goes to refectory, and ask for some comfrey, and we'll give it to him in warm milk."

Valiant loved milk, and never got any unless he stole a drink from the pail when he hoped nobody was looking. Almost anything, Lovel reckoned, could be got down him if it was mixed with milk.

Harding nodded. "I'll get him back to the stable; he'll be best in his own corner."

Lovel found Brother Peter in the infirmary stillroom, measuring out a syrup for Brother Godwyn's cough, and burst out with his request.

"Broken foreleg, eh," said Brother Peter, setting down the measuring glass. "I'm sorry to hear that, very sorry. A good friendly beast, yes, yes, and behaved as reverently as any Christian, the time he got into the church. Comfrey, yes, I think we might spare—"

Brother Eustace's dry voice sounded from the inner doorway, "Brother Peter, may I remind you that nothing is dispensed from the infirmary stillroom without my leave?"

"Yes, yes—of course I would have asked you before—" Brother Peter began guiltily, and his voice trailed away, as the dry one went on.

"The remedies on these shelves are for the healing of men and women and children, not for brute beasts, no matter how christianly they behave themselves in church after they have chased the stable cat halfway up the rood screen!"

"But we have plenty of the infusion, Brother Eustace. Don't you think—"

"That is beside the point," said Brother Eustace, and his voice took on the familiar edge of exasperation. "It's not even as though the animal was a working dog; it's a useless creature anyway."

Lovel suddenly heard a voice that did not seem to be quite his own, saying, "Father Infirmarer, you said that about me, once, but I reckon you've found me useful enough to you these past months."

There was a small sharp silence. Brother Peter watched in dismay as Lovel and the Infirmarer stood looking at each other. Lovel was feeling rather sick, and his heart was racing. There was a little frown between Brother Eustace's eyes. "Did I?" he said at last. "If so, I do not think that you were meant to hear it, and I am sorry. There remains the question of Harding's dog. It is not easy to make a broken bone knit properly in its true position; did you think that it might have been kinder to let Harding finish the animal's suffering at once?"

"Yes," Lovel said; and still the voice did not quite belong to him. "I thought."

"And are you sure that you did not merely do what you wanted to do?"

"Yes," Lovel said again. "I could feel the way the bone was broken and how it ought to go together again."

"You have of course a vast experience in such matters."

Lovel shook his head, trying to explain, "I *felt* it."

There was another silence, and then Brother Eustace said, "Well, you were certainly splinting it in an extremely competent manner."

Lovel's eyes widened. "You saw?"

"I watched you for some time. But you were too deeply occupied to notice anything apart from what you were doing." Suddenly the Infirmarer seemed to make up his mind. He turned to the stocked shelves and took down a jar with a wooden stopper. "There should be enough of the infusion left in this jar to do all you need. I would tell you to leave the splints on until this day month, but doubtless you know that already. When you propose to take them off, will you let me know? I should like to be present."

That night, long after the other monastery servants were asleep, Lovel lay wide awake on his pallet bed at the far end of the dormitory. He felt very much older than when he woke up that morning; and as though something strange and tremendous and rather frightening had happened to him, changing him into a slightly different person, so that he could never go back to being exactly the Lovel he had been before.

VI

THE NOVICE

Kneeling in the stable straw, with the old man-at-arms holding Valiant between his knees, and Brother Eustace looking on from the doorway, Lovel felt sick and his fingers seemed made of wood. The big dog had been trotting around, dot-and-go-one, on three legs almost from the first, and in the past week he had even begun putting the broken foreleg to the ground. But now the month was up; and how would it be when the splints were off? He took up Harding's knife that was lying ready, and began to cut the binding rags. It would be hopeless to try to untie them, they were matted solid with dirt long ago.

The last knot parted; and Lovel drew the bits of wood away, and began to feel the dog's foreleg, while Valiant looked up into his face, whimpering and wagging his tail. He could feel the place where the break had been, the bone a little thickened over the mend; but the join was straight and true. He felt Valiant lick his thumb, and opened his eyes—he had not even known when he shut them so that nothing should interfere with the feeling that was like another kind of sight in his hands. "Up, boy!"

Valiant half obeyed, then checked, missing the familiar support of the splint, and looked at him inquiringly.

"Up!" Lovel said again. "Up, boy! Up, Valiant!"

He struggled up himself, and moved backward a few steps, and whistled as well as he could for the dryness of his mouth. "Come!" And with a protesting whine, Valiant got up. Lovel moved back and whistled again; and Valiant put his right forepaw uncertainly to the ground; one step, two, quite steadily, and then tucked it up again and finished the journey on three legs, to thrust his muzzle into Lovel's hand.

A sickening sense of loss and failure rose in Lovel; bewilderment too; everything had seemed to be going so well, for those first few steps. Then beside him, Brother Eustace stooped and felt the dog's foreleg with a practiced hand. "It's perfectly sound. That's no more than habit."

The old man-at-arms nodded. "Likely he'll go on three legs to the end of his days whenever he wants sympathy or hopes 'twill get him off a hiding." He was grinning with relief all over his red, roughhewn face; he even forgot the respect due to one of the Brethren. "You couldn't have done much better nor that yourself, eh Father Infirmarer?"

Brother Eustace looked up from his examination of Vali-

ant's leg, his face as bleak and his voice as cool and dry
as ever. "No, I believe I could not," he said.

Lovel turned away from them both and from Valiant,
who had sat down to lick his paw, and went across to the
church.

In after years, Lovel was never quite sure how or when
the idea had started, that he should enter the Order.
Whether it was after Valiant, or not until the sickness
broke out among the Brothers the following spring, and
he found himself working in the infirmary day and night
with the Father Infirmarer and Brother Peter.

Probably something would have been said to him about
it sooner, but late in 1121 a great sorrow fell upon all England. For four years past—almost ever since the night that
Rahere had lodged in the Nazareth Chamber—the King
had been overseas, and with him Prince William his heir;
for the boy had received Normandy from King Louis of
France on condition of doing him homage for it, and there
had been many things to arrange and watch over. But at
last all was in order, and a little before Christmas Henry
sailed for England, weighing anchor from Barfleur at
dusk, while Prince William followed in another ship a
few hours later, and many of the young people of the
court, who were his friends and boon-companions, with
him. But the second ship, sailing after dark, struck a rock
and broke up. Only one man got ashore from the wreck,
and he was not the Prince.

Throughout England there was grief and mourning, for

people had hoped great things of the King's son when his time came to rule them; and hardly a great house in the kingdom but had lost son or brother, friend or kinsman. And in New Minster as in every church and cathedral throughout the land, as the weeks turned into months and the time of mourning went by, Solemn Mass followed Solemn Mass for the souls of the young Prince and his friends, whose bodies had never been found. And all other affairs were laid aside.

So it was late summer and Lovel was almost eighteen when the Abbot sent for him and suggested that he should take his vows and become one of the Brethren.

Standing in the Abbot's parlor before the lean, hawk-nosed man who always looked as though he should have been wearing mail rather than the black habit of the Benedictines, Lovel stammered a little. "Father Abbot, I—I had not thought to enter the Order."

"Never once?" said the Abbot.

"It has—drifted into my head once or twice—and out again. I never really thought about it. I am a monastery servant, and well enough content with that."

"We have done more than think about it, my son; we have discussed your case in Chapter. Brother Eustace, Brother Peter and Brother Anselm all feel that you would do well."

"Brother Eustace!" Lovel said, startled.

"It was Brother Eustace who brought the matter up. I

think—" the Abbot smiled—"that he would like to be able
to count on more help in the infirmary. However, that is
not in itself perhaps the best of reasons for entering a
religious order."

So the Father Abbot talked to Lovel of the joys of a life
lived entirely for God; and then bade him go away and
think. And Lovel went away and thought, but not quite
as the Father Abbot had intended.

He knew that the gift of healing was in him from his
grandmother; he felt it every time he touched anything
that was sick or in pain. He knew that he would make a
good physician. It was the one thing he would ever do
well, and the one thing he wanted to do; and though
there were physicians outside the Church, it cost money
to get one to take you on as his boy and teach you all his
skills; and more money to set yourself up afterward. For
a poor man who wanted to heal the sick, so far as he
knew, the Church was the only way. Also—but this he did
not admit even to himself—the thought of leaving the
monastery and going out into the world again frightened
him. The world had not been overkind to him the last
time he was in it. Since then he had been more than six
years within the sheltering walls of New Minster; and
they had come to mean sanctuary to him, especially in
these later years in the physic garden and the infirmary;
even if sometimes they also seemed a little like the walls
of a prison.

He knew that if Rahere with the half-bitter, half-laugh-

ing monk's face had come back and whistled for him, he
would have run out of the monastery gates and away after
him to the world's edge and beyond. But Rahere had never
come back.

So on a soft autumn morning with the thrush singing
his heart out in the elder tree, Lovel put on for the first
time the habit of a Benedictine novice, and with Brother
Peter on one side of him, and Brother Anselm who was
growing very old and tottery on the other, crossed the
cloister garth to the great minster church. But all through
the long ceremony that followed, no matter how hard he
tried to turn his mind and heart to more solemn things,
he heard the thrush singing in the monastery garden.

His days had been full enough before, but now they
became so full that sometimes it seemed that there were
not hours enough between one sunrise and the next. Now
he studied every day with the other novices in the north
walk of the cloister, and instead of the single daily Mass
to which all the work people went, the bell called him
seven times a day to worship; and in whatever time the
other novices were free, there was always Brother Eustace
or Brother John wanting him for the infirmary or the
physic garden.

And then one dreary November day, Brother Anselm
was found slumped unconscious across his reading desk
in the library. They carried him into the monks' warming-
room, and presently he recovered and was as though nothing had happened, laughing at them gently for their

concern. But before November was out, it happened again, and this time he took longer to revive, and seemed dazed and unsure of himself; so they took him to the infirmary and put him in the pallet bed where Lovel himself had lain when he first came to New Minster.

"Let Lovel stay with me for a little while," he said; and then, "I shall be back with you all again tomorrow."

But next morning, when he heard the bell ringing for Prime, and tried to get up, his tired old legs would not carry him; and Lovel, who had snatched a moment to look in on him before the service, helped Brother Peter to get him back into bed, and so arrived late for Prime, and got scolded as though he were about six by the Novice Master, and was ordered to fast at the midday meal, by way of penance.

The old Precentor lay in the pallet bed as the days went by, staring into the chapel where the candles glimmered before the altar, or out of the window at the bare trees in the garden and the old rooks' nests. And every moment that he could snatch, Lovel spent with him—first thing in the dark of the winter mornings, last thing in the dark of the winter nights, a dozen times during the day. They stopped giving him penances for being late for things; indeed the time came when he was given leave to worship in the tiny infirmary chapel instead of attending many of the services in the great minster church. As the old man grew weaker, he seemed only content when Lovel was with him; and Lovel did everything for him—washed him and fed him, prayed with him, and comforted him when he grew confused and did not know quite where he was. There was nothing to be done to make him well again.

"He is not ill," Brother Peter said. "No, no, just old, and worn out with living."

The rooks were building in the trees that you could see from the infirmary windows, and the snowdrops were in flower in the physic garden. And it became clear that Brother Anselm could not live more than a few days longer. Lovel sat beside him one night, wondering what to do because the old man had fallen asleep holding onto his hand like a small child. The candles burned low in the sanctuary, and beyond the windows the rooks' nests made dark blobs against the afterglow. He heard sandaled feet scuffing across the inner cloister, and one of his fellow novices stood in the doorway. "There's a traveler asking for you, and the Father Abbot has given you leave to go to him. Rahere—would that be the name?"

VII

THE KING AND THE BEGGING BOWL

In the silence, the dry light breathing of the Precentor sounded very clear, and he felt the old man's hand light and brittle as a withered leaf in his. "I cannot leave Brother Anselm," he said.

"I am to sit with Brother Anselm till you get back. The Father Abbot said you might have an hour," said the young novice. "He's asleep now, anyway."

Lovel hesitated a moment longer, then very carefully he freed his hand from the old man's and got up. "If he wakes, give him this cup to drink, and tell him that I will soon be back."

He saw his fellow novice take his place, then went out. He went as fast as he could down the long dark slype to the main cloister, and past the monk who sat on duty in the little gate parlor, into the outer courtyard. He turned left toward the Guest Lodging; but the man called after him, "You're going the wrong way. It's the hospice you want."

Lovel looked back, "The hospice? Are you sure?"

"Of course I'm sure," said the other, testily, and returned to reading his breviary.

Lovel hovered doubtfully a moment, then crossed the courtyard to the long barnlike building beside the gate-house, where the poorer kind of travelers were housed.

Sometimes the hospice was crowded to overflowing but this evening there was only one solitary traveler there, standing with his back to the room and looking at the little daubed picture of the Madonna of the Highways, which a traveling artist had painted there years ago in thanks for his night's lodging.

And seeing him, Lovel's heart sank with sick disappointment. This was not Rahere, this unknown man in the black habit of an Austin canon, tattered at the hem and caked to the knee with February mud. There had been some stupid mistake. . . .

And then the man turned around—and there had been no mistake at all.

They stood and looked at each other a few silent moments, and then Rahere's face winged into its old twisted smile. "You find me changed."

"I'm not sure," Lovel said, slowly.

"Not sure?"

"The night I played page for you when you lodged in

the Nazareth Chamber, I *think* you were a minstrel who
was already half a monk. Now—I think you are a church-
man who is still half a jongleur." Lovel broke off in confusion, surprised and rather ashamed of what he had said.

"Bravo! But you I find most surely changed. You have
done a vast deal of growing up."

"You can do a vast deal of growing up in five years,"
Lovel said.

Rahere looked at him with those strange brilliant eyes
that saw so uncomfortably deep. "It isn't only the five
years," he said at last. And then, "They told me when I
asked for you that you were about your duties in the infirmary. I take it that you no longer do all the odd jobs
that nobody else wants to do."

"No, only the ones that the Father Infirmarer doesn't,"
Lovel said with the ghost of a grin. "But I wasn't about
any duties, I was just sitting with Brother Anselm. He's
very ill." Then remembering Brother Peter, "Well no, not
ill; but very old and worn out. He's asleep now, and one
of the other novices is sitting with him, so that I could
come to you. But I must go back soon."

"Meanwhile, sit and keep me company while I eat my
supper," said Rahere, as the Father Hospitaler entered
with a novice carrying a bowl of fish broth and a loaf of
dark rye bread.

So when they were alone again, Lovel drew a stool to
the end of the long trestle-table, and sat down. He did not
attempt to serve Rahere as he had done before; that had

belonged to the Nazareth Chamber and the silver and fine linen. This was something different. Watching the other while he ate, Lovel thought that he looked ill, or as though he had quite lately been ill. His face was all sharp angles, the yellowish skin lying lightly over the bones, with no flesh between; his eyes sunk deep into his head. But the old sparkle was there, the old wicked laughter over the old sadness; only, Lovel realized suddenly, the sadness had deepened and lost the bitterness that had been mixed with it; and so had the laughter. He had been wrong when he had thought that Rahere had not changed, and he wondered what had changed him.

Rahere's mouth quirked suddenly in amusement, and he said in the old soft drawl, as though Lovel had spoken his thoughts out loud, "Would it not be enough if I said that life became quite unbearably dull and dreary at court after the White Ship went down, and I felt that it was time to make a change?"

"No," Lovel said, "it wouldn't."

"Then I must try again." But Rahere was silent for a long time, making bread pellets and dropping them into his empty soup bowl. At last he looked up. "It already seemed to me, five years ago, that there must be something more to life than making the King laugh after supper—either that, or life was such a small and unimportant matter that the only thing for a sensible man to do was to wear it as lightly as a feather in his bonnet—play with it like a jingle of fool's bells. . . . I was with the King in

Normandy those four years—did you wonder why I never came back? When we were at Barfleur and on the point of sailing for England, the Prince bade me to wait and sail with him and his fellows. The voyage, he said, would not be so merry without Rahere to set the tune. They were all in wild spirits. I refused, for no good reason save that I was not, and sailed with the King instead." He got up, and walked the length of the long room and back. "The Prince was just about your age, Brat; few of them were much older. I'd seen them grow up."

Rahere sat down and began making bread pellets again; and again Lovel waited, patiently, for him to go on.

"It seemed to me then that if life was indeed a small matter, there could be no God to trouble Himself with such a trifle; and I found, somewhat to my surprise, that I could not believe there was no God. It followed then, that there was something more to life than making the King laugh after supper—which is as well, for the King is not one for laughter these days. Do I make sense to you? I am none so sure that I do to myself."

"I think so," Lovel said. "So you set out to find it—this something more."

"I did. But when I had taken this—" Rahere touched his dusty black habit—"I felt that there should be something yet more, to mark the end of one life and the beginning of another. My artist's soul demanded it." He was mocking at himself now. "Hi My! I have all the jongleur's instinct for the right dramatic gesture that is not only for the audience but the thing within oneself. I still make sense?"

Lovel nodded.

"There have been kings who have laid aside their crowns and taken up the begging bowl; and for a king that is gesture enough; but hardly for a king's jongleur. So to tidy up the raveled ends of my old life and make ready for the new, I went on pilgrimage to Rome. It was like to be the start of a new life indeed, for at the Three Fountains there, I caught some foul fever which lurks there, and was, so the good Brothers who nursed me told me, very like to die—the which was no good news to me. And I had no wish to die in Rome. We are told that it is a blessed thing to die on pilgrimage, but I—my grand-father was a Breton, following Richard de Belmain in the Conqueror's Army, but I am London born and bred, even as de Belmain's son who is Bishop of London now, and was fain to see my own land and my own city again. So when I began to mend, I made a vow in thanks-offer-ing, that when I came to my own place again, I would raise an infirmary, a hospital for the poor sick, that in London poor men might be cared for as I had been in Rome."

Again Lovel nodded, his eyes never leaving Rahere's face.

"Just the hospital, you understand, but on my way home I had a vision." Rahere said it as another man might say that he had found a penny or his horse had cast a shoe.

"It was a very hot night, which is odd when one comes to think of it, for my sickness had held me long in Rome and it was close on Christmastime, and I could not sleep. I lay tossing about trying both to get cool and to think whereabouts, in or near London, I might find the land I needed to build my hospital. Then it seemed to me suddenly that the room and all things about me dissolved away, and I saw coming toward me a great beast with eight legs and eagle's wings. It caught me in its talons and lifted me up among the stars. If anyone ever asks you, you may tell them with my compliments that the stars do not merely twinkle; at close quarters they spin round and round upon themselves giving off a high singing sound and a strong smell of feverfew. Below me there was nothing but blackness, and I knew that in the next instant the beast would loose its hold and I should plunge down into blackness and falling that would last for all eternity. I cried out; and Saint Bartholomew came in at the door—oh a most respectable and dignified old body with a beard as long and white as the Milky Way—and told me that I should build the hospital at Smithfield, just outside London Walls. They have a horse-market there once a week—I've been out to it often. He bade me also to build a priory beside the hospital. And with that I fell asleep. And when I woke in the morning I was cold rather than hot; and small wonder, with the snow on the ground." Rahere rubbed his long blue chin. "The odd thing is that I had been thinking of Smithfield before, but it is the King's land, and Our Henry is not one to care greatly about the sick poor. But a priory is another matter, and with Saint Bartholomew for good measure . . ."

"You think he will really give you the land?"

Rahere smiled gently. "Our Henry is mean, but devout. Saint Bartholomew will have his priory; but the hospital comes first."

Silence settled between them again, and they looked at each other across the corner of the table and Rahere's soup-bowl with its mess of bread pellets in the bottom. Lovel had a fairly shrewd idea that he knew this sickness. It was a fever that breathed from marshy, mosquito-ridden places in hot weather. And often, when the main attack was spent, if the one who had it lived, it returned from time to time, bringing cold and great heat and strange waking dreams.

He had a feeling that Rahere had some inkling of this, and perhaps only half-believed in his vision; surely if he had quite believed he would have told the story in a different way—or maybe not. Another man would, but then another man was not Rahere. Only one thing was certain —that vision or fever-dream had shown Rahere how to get the land he needed from the King; and that however it had come he believed in the message and was grateful for it. How Rahere was going to build a hospital, let alone a priory, Lovel could not imagine, but seeing the brilliant eyes and faintly mocking, resolute mouth, he did not doubt that, somehow, Rahere would do it.

And suddenly he ached to be going with him, to help him do the impossible.

He got up. "I was given an hour, and I think that I have been longer. I must go back to Brother Anselm."

Next morning after High Mass, he was with Rahere again, walking to and fro in the inner cloister close to the infirmary. Already the buds of the fig tree against the wall were swelling, and he could hear the thrush trying over the first notes of the year.

"Come with me," Rahere said. "I'll need your skill."

All night long, as he drowsed and woke beside Brother Anselm's bed, Lovel had been thinking of Rahere saying that. But now he felt as unprepared as though he had not thought of it at all; and two waves of feeling surged over him, so close upon each other that they were almost one. The first was a great lift of the heart, a longing to go with Rahere who had come back and whistled for him after all. The second was fear; fear of the world outside the monastery walls, where men had driven him away with stones, a witch's brat, because he was made crooked instead of straight like other men. But the longing was stronger than the fear.

Then he shook his head. "I cannot."

"You're still only a novice, you're perfectly free."

"I can't leave Brother Anselm," Lovel said. "Not now. He is not happy with anyone but me to do things for him; and he cannot live more than a few days longer."

"And I cannot wait," Rahere said. "I must push on about the business that has been entrusted to me."

Lovel nodded. They had stopped walking and were standing at the arched doorway into the slype.

"You wish to come, I think?" Rahere said.

"With all my heart."

"And you say that he can live only a few more days.

Think, Lovel, are you prepared to trade your whole life for an old man's few days?"

"Yes," Lovel said after a moment; and saying it seemed to tear at something deep within his chest.

"You'll make an infirmarer, one day," Rahere said. "God keep you, Brother Brat."

And he turned and went with that long light step of his along the slype toward the main cloister and the outer court.

Lovel looked after him for a moment, then turned also and went limping back to the infirmary.

VIII

THE ROAD TO LONDON

Just a week later, Brother Anselm died. The old body was laid in the monks' graveyard, and the pallet bed at the end of the Infirmary Hall was first neatly and coldly empty, and then bulgingly overful of Brother Dominic with the black colic. And Lovel was left in a sort of private wilderness, wondering whether he had been a complete fool after all; especially as Brother Anselm had slept almost all the time through that last week, anyway. But when he went to the library to look up something in the great herb book, it fell open at the page with the drawing of comfrey on it. And then he did not wonder anymore.

Spring drew on toward summer, and on the minster farm they got in the hay, and then the corn; and it was

drawing on to the end of Lovel's year as a novice, and
the time for him to take his final vows.

And then one day the Father Abbot sent for him again.

Lovel hurriedly brushed himself down and straightened
his habit, for there was no one in the infirmary just then
and he was back at his old work with Brother John in
the physic garden; and went to answer the summons,
rummaging in his mind as he went for any misdeed or
duty left undone.

But when he stood before the Father Abbot, he realized
with relief that it was not that kind of summons at all.

The Father Abbot sat back in his great carved chair
and looked at him consideringly down his great hooked
nose. "My son, when our good Brother Rahere last came
this way, he asked my leave to take you from us, if you
wished to go with him. I gather that he asked you, and
that you refused."

"Brother Anselm was still in this life. I could not leave
him, Father."

The Abbot nodded. "So if the thing returned to you
again, you would go?"

"Yes, Father Abbot."

"I thought so." The Abbot sat up. "This morning I received a letter from Rahere, asking that if you are free
now and wish it, you should be allowed to join him."

"Where, Father?" said Lovel. It was the only question
that needed asking.

"At a place just outside London Walls. Smithfield, they

call it." The Abbot smiled. "He bids me tell you that if you ask for Smithfield where they hold the weekly horse fair, anybody will tell you the way."

"I may go then, Father?" Lovel said, wanting to get that clearly fixed amid the joyful confusion in his head.

"My son, you are yet a novice, and free to go where or when you will, without my leave. Go with my blessing instead."

Three days later, Lovel stood outside the minster gates; the first time, except for a few visits to the farm, that he had passed through them in nearly eight years.

He had the habit he stood up in, a little money that the almoner had given him for the journey in his scrip, along with a barley loaf, and a sprig of rue from the physic garden; a stout ash staff to help his lame leg, and before him the long road to London.

"Follow the road that goes *that* way, and don't go branching off, and you're safe to come to London Bridge in the end," Harding had told him. "But if you'd any sense in your head you'd not be going. Valiant'll miss you sore."

A surprising number of the Brothers and the monastery servants had seemed sorry that he was going, the Father Infirmarer among them; their God speeds were still in his ears, and the loving thrust of Valiant's muzzle still in his hand. Behind him in the shadow of the gate arch the monastery gates stood open as they always did in the day-

time; and for a moment he was within a hair's breadth of
turning back through them again, back from the strange
world where men threw stones, into the familiar sanctuary.

But he knew that if he did that, he would have failed
Rahere, and failed something deep within himself that
men generally called their soul.

He turned his face toward London and started walking.

IX

THE BEGINNING OF A DREAM

The road to London was white with the dust of August.
It lay thick over the hedgerows, turning grass and bushes
and the tattered wayside tangle of ragwort and hardheads
and yarrow to pale ghosts of themselves, and rose in chok-
ing clouds under the feet of the passersby.

There were many passersby, coming and going, up to
London and down to Winchester and the great seaport
town beyond. A river of people, it had often seemed to
Lovel in the past, watching it flow by the Abbey gateway
and sometimes come eddying in and out again. But then
he had been safe, like someone standing on the bank and
watching the river hurry by. Now he had let go his safety
and pushed out into midstream, and he felt strange and
frightened and a bit like a lost dog.

So many people, and all with strangers' faces . . . Even
in the monasteries where he lodged each night, where the
life was the kind he knew, the Brothers all had strangers'

faces; all eyes and mouths, like the people in the old evil
dreams that had ended with stones whistling round his
ears. Part of him longed for the quiet of the familiar
cloisters and the herbs growing in the physic garden that
would surely not grow as well for anybody else as they had
for him; and once or twice he was very near to turning
back. But ahead of him was London, and Rahere who had
whistled for him to come and help make an impossible
dream come true. And that kept him going, day after
weary day, in the right direction.

His leg made him a slow traveler, and once or twice he
even had to lie up for a day to rest it before taking to the
road again; and so it was Saint Bartholomew's Eve, August
almost turning into September, when he came at last to
London Bridge.

He was red-eyed and powdered thick with wayside dust,
and his twisted foot had rubbed itself raw and bleeding
under the chafing sandal strap; and the road from Winchester that had always seemed to him like a river, had
become suddenly a river in roaring spate. He was shoul-
dered to the wall by a knot of horsemen, and stood there
for a while, watching the crowd go by, and trying to
nerve himself to push out into it again. Merchants passed
him with strings of packhorses; country folk bringing up
farm stuff for the markets; a drover with a herd of lowing
bullocks. They looked, Lovel thought, almost as tired and
bewildered as himself, with strings of slime hanging from
their soft muzzles; a knight in a leather hauberk freckled

with rust spots from his mail; a pilgrim with scallop shells in his hat to show that he had been all the way to the shrine of Saint James at Compostella; a little wizened old woman in a horse litter with mounted servants riding before her to clear the way; beggars and craftsmen and men-at-arms, flocking into and out of London by the one narrow wooden bridge.

Well, it was no good to stand here all day; the sun was well over toward the west, and he still had to find Smith-field. Lovel took a deep breath, tightened his hold on his staff, and plunged once more into the jammed and jostling throng.

Soon he was out on the bridge, his footsteps and all those other footsteps turning hollow on the timber-way, and the whole bridge thrumming like a harp-string under-foot with the rush of the great river against its piers. He passed the little bridge chapel, dropping his toll penny into the hand of the wizened old Benedictine Brother in charge; and at last reached the other side, where the crowd thinned out again as it branched away into different streets.

Lovel heaved a sigh of relief, and looked about for some-one to tell him the way to Smithfield. There were people everywhere, but they all seemed in much too great a hurry to be able to tell anybody the way to anywhere. At last he found one citizen who did not seem to be going anywhere or doing anything special; a very fat man with a sprig of honeysuckle in his belt, propping up the front of a corn-

chandler's shop, and watching the gulls and the fisher-boats along the quayside as though he had all day to do it in, and all tomorrow too, if need be.

"Smithfield is it?" said the man. "Well now, if you follow Fish Street—that's the steep one yonder up the hill —and then turn off to the left along Candlewick Street to Paul's Churchyard, pass the Folk Moot, and go down the Shambles, that'll bring you to the New Gate. Look for the Church of Saint Sepulchre's, just outside the city walls, and take the turning to the right, just past it, and keep straight on for a bit, down the road, and if you haven't had your throat cut by pickpurses, Reverend Brother, you're there."

"I don't think I'd be worth any pickpurse's while," Lovel said, not quite sure whether to take one word of this seriously, and finding it hard to think straight, in so much noise and bustle.

"You don't know our pickpurses, you being, as I'd guess, from distant parts," said the fat man darkly. "No respect for the Church, they haven't, and they'd strangle their own grandmothers for the price of her Sunday kerchief!" And then, seeing Lovel's tired and bewildered face, he dropped the joke, and said kindly enough, "If 'twas me, when I got to New Gate I'd just look for a big crowd all going one way, and follow along. That way you can't miss it."

"And this crowd—why would it be going to Smith-field?" Lovel was finding it harder and harder to think

straight. "I was told that the horse-market was on Satur-
days, and surely this is only Wednesday?"

"Wednesday as ever is," said the man reassuringly, now
clearly deciding that Lovel was lacking in the head as
well as all else. "They'd be going to Saint Bartholomew's
Fair. That's a great new cloth-fair that the King has given
leave to be held there. A three-day fair, and all the fair
dues are going to help pay for building a hospital and a
fine new priory for the good of the King's soul! You just
go along with the crowd, and you can't miss it."

Lovel remembered Rahere saying that Henry was mean
but devout, and he thought with a small warm flicker of
laughter in the midst of all his weariness, that Rahere had
used his vision well. He thanked the man, and was just
turning away when the other was struck by an idea.

"They've only just started building, as I hear; if it's a
miracle you're wanting, best go back to wherever you
came from, and wait a bit."

"There's miracles and miracles," Lovel said, not knowing quite what he meant. "I think I'll go on, all the same."

And he set off up the steep slope of Fish Street.

He found the turning into Candlewick Street, and
presently came out by a big church in an open space, that
a man carrying a cadge of falcons told him was Saint Paul's;
and after that it wasn't hard to find the Shambles by the
smell of blood and the carcasses hanging everywhere outside the butchers' stalls. Certainly by that time, the crowd
was growing thick again, and mostly heading one way.

So he took the fat man's advice, and simply went with the flow.

He was so tired and hungry that everything had begun to seem like a dream, and the gable-ends of the tall houses that fronted the streets had become fantastic faces that watched him with windows for eyes. Then there was a gateway, like a dark, gaping throat, and then the houses dwindled and there was another church which he supposed vaguely must be Saint Sepulchre's. And then at last, there was a glimpse of open country, with the shadows lying long and cool in the westering sunlight.

But ahead of him there began to be a new buzz and hum and worry of sound; and suddenly, with marshy grass under his feet, Lovel found himself on the edge of what seemed to be another city. A city of painted wooden booths and many-colored tents, all set out in streets, and the streets even more throng-full of people than the streets of London had been.

Almost at once he was lost. Streets of cloth merchants melted into streets of shoemakers and leather merchants which faded in turn into a street of gold- and silversmiths; and all around, in every bit of open space, were sellers of apples and gilt gingerbread, fortune-tellers, acrobats in spangled tights; once, a mangy bear, dancing sadly to the tune its keeper played on a whistle-pipe. Lovel felt for it as a brother; it looked so sad and bewildered, and on its hind legs it was such a clumsy shape.

Presently, without quite knowing how he got there, he

came to the far edge of the fairground, and saw in front
of him open space and evening light, sour grass churned
up into mud underfoot, piles of stone and timber lying
about, a cluster of wooden lodges with roofs of hurdles
and reed-thatch rough and shaggy as an old hill-ram's
fleece, and in the midst of all, the walls of a long building
standing shoulder-high, raw with newness in the sunset
light—and workmen everywhere, going about their jobs
or leaning on their tools to watch other people working.

The beginning of Rahere's dream!

Lovel stood and gazed, not knowing quite what to do
next, and feeling a little like someone who has come home
from a long journey but isn't sure of the way in. Somewhere among those rough bothies he supposed that he
would find Rahere; but suddenly it was more than he
could do, to go forward and start the last bit of his search.

And as he stood there, leaning on his staff, he heard a
startling fluting close behind him, and for an instant he
was back in the Nazareth Chamber at New Abbey. He
turned around clumsily, and there, with his black habit
kilted up through his belt as he had used to wear his
riding tunic, stood Rahere!

Relief flooded over Lovel, and suddenly everything
shone as it does when the sun breaks through a rift in
the clouds on a wet day.

"So you came," Rahere said.

"Brother Anselm died the week after you were at the
Abbey."

"And so it seemed good to you to follow when I whistled, after all."

"It seemed—very good," Lovel said; and then, "You know how greatly I wanted to, before; but I couldn't leave Brother Anselm while he still needed me."

Around them, everything was a roaring, many-colored dream, but in the middle of the dream it was very quiet, and Lovel and Rahere stood and looked at each other, quite alone to themselves. Then Rahere reached out, the black sleeves of his habit falling back from his big bony hands, and touched the extreme tip of a long forefinger down onto each of Lovel's shoulders, just as he had done that long ago stormy evening in the Nazareth Chamber.

"You couldn't leave Brother Anselm," he agreed. "What a ridiculous and contrariwise thing is the soul of man. If you could have left Brother Anselm—oh, I would have taken you gladly for your skill with pills and poultices; but you can have no idea, Brother Brat, how disappointed I should have been!"

X

SAINT BARTHOLOMEW'S HOSPITAL

Smithfield, "The Smooth Field," was the open land between London Wall and the Fleet River. Beside the great Saturday horse-markets, it was used for games and horse racing; part of it was a market, where people brought in their cattle and sheep and pigs, and in another part of it, criminals were hanged. And it was all cut up by feet and hooves and wheels until it looked like a marsh. Not a very likely place to be building a priory and a hospital, seemingly; but under the mud and the sour trampled grass was good solid ground, and the water of the springs near the river was clean and pure.

"Saint Bartholomew," Rahere said to Lovel the day after he arrived, "must have a quite remarkable eye for land."

Lovel did just wonder whether it was Saint Bartholomew who had the eye for land, or the Austin canon who had once been the King's Jongleur. But when he glanced around at the lean black cranefly figure beside him, there

was nothing in Rahere's pale bright eyes but reflected sunlight, as he cocked his head on one side and whistled
companionably to a speckled starling gobbling crumbs
where the workmen had eaten their midday meal.

There were quite a lot of workmen on the hospital by
now; mostly laborers and course-setters, but a few free
masons—skilled men who could trim up stone to a perfect
fit and carve a chevron arch-molding, and carried themselves as greater than other men accordingly. But beside
these, there were men who had come in to help the work
along, simply because Rahere wanted them. Rahere the
preacher could play on his hearers as Rahere the King's
Jongleur could play on his lute, and every time he went
out to preach in some city church, men would come to
him afterward with offers of help, even if it was only a
single day's help that they could spare from their proper
trade. And their proper trades were of every kind known
to the city and the country around. Once there was even
a pickpurse who remained honest for one whole day.
Quite often there were young squires whose trade was
simply that they were learning to be knights, who would
strip off their good embroidered tunics and set to in their
shirts and hose with the best will in the world.

Those were the ones that drove Beornfred, the Master
Mason, to the brink of distraction.

"Have a little patience, my gentle flower of all master
builders," Lovel heard Rahere saying to him one day.
"Think how good it is for your soul as well as theirs."

"But they don't know how to lay a course," Beornfred had almost howled, his weather-burned face puckered like a baby's when it is going to cry. "This wall, this whole fine hospital of yours is going to fall down if a cat breathes on it!"

And Rahere had turned and laid one long finger experimentally against a squat stone buttress, and said in a tone as soothing as run honey, "It seems quite strong."

As the months went by, the new life folded itself around Lovel as once the old life had done. It was a life that centered, for him, and he thought for Rahere too, not so much in the cleared and leveled space marked out with stakes into the ground-pattern of the priory church that would rise there one day, but in the hospital house that was already taking shape nearby. The two long wards with the central hearth where they joined, and the little altar chapel where the Master already held the daily Mass though there was no one yet to come to it except Lovel and sometimes a handful of workmen; and no roof but a few hurdles above the altar.

The hospital house was stone built as the church would be, but all around it were low wattle-and-daub buildings (not very different, except that they were smaller, from the masons' lodges), that would be kitchens and outhouses and the lodgings of the Master and Brothers one day. And on the one clear side of it, looking south toward the city wall, Lovel had begun before he had been at Smithfield three days, to make his physic garden.

Three old elder-trees grew on that side of the hospital, and he took care to enclose them within the rough wattle fence that was to keep stray animals out. And as the months went by, with whatever help he could get, and often with no help at all, he cleared the scrub and dug the ground over so that the frost could get at it later. Already, in his head, he saw his garden laid out in neat plots with narrow paths between, stocked and beautiful with all the herbs and simples that he had tended with Brother John in the physic garden at New Minster. Foxglove and celandine, comfrey and rue . . . Already in a few carefully prepared patches, he had plants and cuttings coming on—presents from other monastery gardens, to be nursed through the winter under straw, and wild things from field and wood and hedgerow of the surrounding countryside. One of the very first herbs he planted, with an apologetic thought toward Brother John, was the pinkish white yarrow that he found beside the track to Clerkenwell. Nothing that was so good for an inflamed wound could belong to the Devil, he was quite sure, whatever Brother John had said; but to be on the safe side, he recited one of his grandmother's herb-gathering charms over it, as he carefully loosened the earth from around the roots:

> Hallowed be thou, Yarrow,
> On the ground thou growest,
> For on the Mount of Calvary

There thou wast found.
Thou healest our Savior Jesus Christ
And staunchest the bleeding wound—

Carefully, he lifted the first root, with a good ball of earth to it.

In the name of the Father, the Son
and the Holy Ghost
I take thee from the ground.

If it *were* the Devil's after all, now it would wither and turn black and stinking in his hands. He looked at it rather anxiously, but the gray-green leaves and flat pannicles of little whitish flowers remained as fresh as ever.

He dug several more, and carried them back to the waiting plot that he had prepared for them, and planted them with as much care as though they had been the balm of Gilead itself. That was when he felt that his physic garden was really born.

But before autumn turned to winter, long before the hospital was finished, Lovel found himself with people to tend as well as plants. It began with an old, old man whose family simply left him on the threshold like an unwanted baby. Then there was a foreign seaman who had been stabbed in a tavern brawl. Then a woman with a baby in her arms, who she said was very sick, and begged Lovel

to make well again; but it was the woman who was sick. The baby was dead.

They buried the baby, and Lovel planted a white briar slip to mark the place, and they looked after the woman until she was well again. The seaman got better and went off vowing vengeance on the man who had stabbed him. The old man died and was buried beside the baby. But by that time others had begun to drift in, piteous and hopeful, asking to be made well again, or at least to be allowed to die in shelter with kindly people around them. And Rahere would turn no one away. So Saint Bartholomew's had become a living hospital, with two more Brothers now to care for the sick, with food boiling in the kitchen and candles burning in the chapel, while the roof was still a makeshift affair of hurdles and thatch that let in the drafts and the winter rain.

On a day at the edge of spring, when the first yellow celandines were opening their eyes in the physic garden, Lovel took his final vows as an Austin canon, before Richard de Belmain, Bishop of London.

He would much sooner have taken them before Rahere; but when he said so, Rahere had smiled his swift, winged smile. "Once a king and his page, now a knight and his squire? It takes a bishop to make a canon, Brother Brat, and I am not even a prior, though I have solemn forebodings that I may blossom into one in some future year." He glanced toward the low line of stone footings where one day the priory church would rise. "But now—I am the Master of Saint Bartholomew's Hospital, no more. It is not in my hands to make a knight out of my squire. So I shall stand beside you while you make your vows before His Grace, the Bishop of London, when he comes to see the progress of the work next month."

So Lovel, with Rahere on one side of him and Master Alfwine who had come to join them from building Saint Giles' at Cripplegate on the other, took his vows in the little bare hospital chapel, before Richard de Belmain.

Only the day before, they had finished the roof and the workmen had stuck up on the gable-end the little decorated tree that announced the fact joyously to the world.

XI

THE PROMISE

Nearly three years went by since Lovel had left the New Minster and set out for London to help Rahere make an impossible dream come true. And it seemed as though the hospital had stood there with its doors open for all who needed it for as long as there had been alders growing by the Fleet River. There were eight Brothers now, and four Sisters, to tend the sick folk in the two long wards, but none of them had Lovel's knowledge of herbs, nor the strange healing power of the hands that had come to him from his grandmother. So the physic garden was still his, and the dispensary that opened from the end of the hospital hall, with its ranged jars and pots and bundles of dried herbs. And he did not sleep in the long lime-washed dormer with the rest of the Brothers, but on a truckle-bed in the corner of the dispensary, so that he was always close at hand if he should be needed in the night.

Most of the folk who came into the hospital or were brought in by their friends, were old, so old or so sick that there was not much to be done for them, except treat them kindly. Lovel did that. With the rest of the Brothers, he took his turn at going out with a handcart to beg food for them so that they should not go hungry. He nursed them, getting used to the sour sick smell of oldness and filth. He listened to them when they wanted to talk, comforted them when they were frightened or miserable, prayed with them and did what he could to ease their aches and pains.

He knew that he was doing the one thing in the world that he was good at; and yet—something was lacking. He didn't notice it at first. But sometimes, at night when he was too tired to sleep, he began to remember from his childhood, Brother Eustace's dry impatient voice, "For an infirmarer there are two ways. One is to bleed a little of your own life away with every sick soul who passes through your hands. The other is to do all that may be done for the sick, but to stand well back while doing it. That way you don't break your heart."

Lovel began to feel that he was doing just that—doing all he could, but standing back. And he didn't want it to be like that; with all his heart and soul he didn't want it to be like that. But could one choose? He prayed about it, but he had never been very good at prayer, and a queer kind of desolation began to grow inside him; a doubt of himself, and a doubt whether God really meant him to heal sick people after all.

He lived with the doubt for quite a long time, until at last something happened that sent him, next day, to find Rahere in the Master's Lodging where he sat battling with the hospital's accounts.

Rahere put aside the accounts without even sighing, and listened to Lovel's doubts as to whether God really meant him to be doctoring the sick at all. And then he said, "Brother Brat, if it is only hands and head with you, then I think for the present hands and head are enough. I could not ask for a better infirmarer; and if God could, then I think He will give you whatever more you need, when the right time comes."

"That is—if He does mean me to be a healer," Lovel said. He took a deep breath. "Master, since yesterday I have doubted that still more. I—crooked as I am—I can't be much of an encouragement to the people I try to help."

"I wonder," Rahere said, and then, "What happened yesterday?"

"I was called to that laborer—the one who put his shoulder out stacking timber when the load slipped. He didn't want me to touch him. He said why didn't I do something about my own shoulder before I made hay with his."

"You put it in again for him, all the same, didn't you," Rahere said simply, his chin propped between his long bony hands, his pale bright eyes never leaving Lovel's face, "and I imagine he feels rather differently about both your shoulder and his, today. . . . Hi My! I am being no help, am I? But what help could you hope for from a king's fool turned cleric? You must find the way for yourself, with God's help, not mine, Brother Brat."

That was in the summer. A day came in early autumn that seemed at first like any other day, except that it was a little less busy than most. There was nobody very ill, the garden was well in hand, and Lovel, pushing the stopper into the last jar of his new decoction of hoarhound and dill, found himself with a little time to spare, if he went without his midday meal. It was not, here, as it was in the rigidly ordered life of the big abbeys; with so many of the Brothers at work or out begging or with sick folk to tend, you could always skip a meal if you wanted to— which was just as well, Lovel thought, because Sister Gertruda was no cook, and when it was her turn to take charge in the kitchen, as it was today, there would be lumps in everything that could have lumps in it, and everything else would be burned to a crisp.

Somebody else was skipping dinner too, for as Lovel made his way down the long ward, taking a quick look from side to side as he went, to make sure that all was well, he saw Brother Luke at work in the little chapel.

Brother Luke was a huge quiet man; one of those people who seem to drift about like a cloud, doing nothing in particular; and yet somehow at the end of the day he would have got through more work than Brother Anders and Brother Dominic put together. And however much he did, he always seemed to have time to spare for more. It was Brother Luke who always had time to sit with anyone who was especially sick, who always had time to help Lovel dig the physic garden, or watch something boiling in the dispensary to see that it didn't boil over. It was Brother Luke, a sign-painter in his young days, who had now brought out his old skill, to paint a picture of Saint Bartholomew behind the altar in the hospital chapel.

Several of the patients who could leave their beds had gathered round to watch—it is always interesting to watch other people at work—and Lovel stopped for a moment to watch too. The picture itself was finished; very bright, like the shop signs that Brother Luke had painted so often to hang out over the street and catch the attention of passersby; and showed the Saint with a long white beard, wearing a blue tunic under a bright pink and red striped cloak, holding a model of the priory in one hand and with the other raised in blessing. He was standing in a garden, and looking, as Rahere had described him in his vision, like a very respectable and dignified old body. And because Brother Luke loved his work and could not bear to waste any corner of it, every inch of the background was full of little clumps of flowers with birds and butterflies hovering over them and beetles climbing up their stalks, and small fat clouds and turning stars and the pointed roofs and tower-tops of distant cities. So, the picture itself was finished, even to the gold halo rather like a straw hat behind the Saint's head. And Brother Luke was painting away carefully at the lettering on a scroll held by two crimson-winged angels underneath.

"For the Lord shall comfort Zion," Lovel read. "He will comfort all her waste places, and He will make her wilderness like Eden, and her desert like the garden of the Lord; joy and gladness shall be found therein, thanksgiving and the voice of melody."

Lovel had seen the words there for two days, drawn out and ready for painting. But they looked different now, with Brother Luke's big hands bringing them to life. They made him think how this place had changed in the three years that Rahere's dream had been growing out of the rough ground of Smithfield; they made him think of his physic garden with the three sentinel elder trees. A promise, he thought, a promise of so many things to so many people, himself not forgotten among them.

Brother Luke looked around and saw him watching and said, "I have made it especially full, so that there will always be plenty for our sick folk to look at—nicer than just the hospital walls."

"Couldn't you find space for just one grass blade more?" Brother Luke never minded being laughed at.

The big man sat back on his heels and looked gravely at his picture, then nodded, and took another brush dipped in yellow paint, and carefully and lovingly painted a sulphur butterfly perching on the very edge of the scroll itself.

For an instant a half-memory brushed across Lovel's mind; something to do with a yellow butterfly and a promise. . . . Then Rahere's voice behind him said, "Perfection! I am convinced that until this moment Our Lord must have found one butterfly too few in that picture!"

And the half-memory slipped back to where it had come from.

And a few moments later, parting from the Master on the hospital doorsill, Lovel went his way.

Ahead of him he could see the choir of the priory church, the strength and beauty of it rising up to cut its proud shape against the sky. There was only the choir as yet, with the rest to follow after, so that the Brothers would not have to wait for the whole church to be built before they could begin to worship God in it.

At a little distance the building seemed remote and not quite real, but as Lovel drew nearer, it grew real and solid and tough and enduring. The men were just getting back to work after their own midday meal, and the whole site was beginning to hum with sound and movement like a swarming hive. Lovel passed the long shed where the Master Mason kept his plans drawn out on plastered boards, dodged a cart loaded with cut stone, and made his way over the rough, churned ground where the carpenters were at work shaping up the great roof beams. In another place the blacksmiths were at work, making rods and clamps and dowels for the vaulting. And from the choir itself, where the big hoist was working, came the shouts of the men sweating at the great wheel that swung the cut stones skyward, and the men high overhead on the hurdle-walks, waiting to receive the swinging ashlars and guide them into place.

Beside the outside hearth in front of one of the masons' lodges, where the men had just been at their dinner, a lanky redheaded boy of about sixteen sat on a balk of timber, finishing up the remains of a big stirabout pot on his knees. He was wiping a long finger round and round inside the pot, and sucking off the blobs of stirabout. But he was not looking at what he was doing, he was gazing up at the tall mass of the choir with the blue sky shining through its clerestory windows.

Lovel never knew, afterward, quite what made him pause in passing; he had never seen the boy before, but it was as though something in him recognized a kind of kinship between them. His shadow fell across the stir-about pot, and the boy looked around with a start; then seeing his black habit, made to get up, awkwardly, as though he was hampered by the big pot on his knees.

Lovel shook his head, and sat down on the balk of tim-ber beside him, stretching out his crooked leg, which was aching as it often did with too much standing on it; and the boy stayed where he was and looked at him, surprised. After a moment he grinned, showing a missing tooth, and then turned grave again. He had a grave face between the laughter.

"You're new on the site, aren't you?" Lovel said.

"Aye. I'm the new scullion as you might say. The dogs-body, the stirabout boy."

Lovel nodded. Every building site had its odd hangers-on of that sort; boys or old men who brewed up the broth and fetched and carried for everybody. Sometimes they were a kinsman of someone among the laborers, some-times a boy learning his trade the hard way, sometimes just a stray out of nowhere and going nowhere. Lovel found himself wanting to know about this boy, but there was something in his freckled face despite the grin that made him feel that asking questions would be like pushing open somebody's door and walking in without asking leave. Instead he said, "I have had no dinner, will you give me a turn at that pot?"

The boy held it out to him. "You are most welcome, Reverend."

And Lovel dipped in a hand and brought out a blob of stirabout on his finger. It was almost cold, thick and slabby, but not burned and with no lumps in it. "This is good. I wish you would come and cook for us in the hospital kitchen," he said, half in earnest.

"I belong here—"the boy jerked his chin toward where the walls of the choir rose into the sunlight with the swal-lows darting to and fro about it, beginning to gather for the autumn flight south—"where there's the walls going up."

It seemed somehow an odd thing to say, for someone who had only just come to Smithfield. But Lovel had

scarcely time to notice, for at that moment someone hidden from view round the side of the forge hut nearby let
out a shout, "Hi! Nick! Nick Redpoll! If you've naught
better to do, come and take a turn at the bellows! Do you
expect me to forge clamps to the Glory of God, *and* keep
the plaguey forge fire going at the same time?"

The boy put down the stirabout pot, which Lovel had
returned to him, and leaned sideways to reach for something half-hidden in the docks and long grass. And Lovel
saw that it was a roughly made crutch, and that Nick Redpoll's left knee was stiff and bent, so that when he stood
up his foot could not reach the ground; and he understood the odd sense of kinship that he had felt for the
redheaded boy.

Watching him hobble off in answer to another yell from
the forge hut, Lovel was reminded sharply of his own
early days at the New Abbey, when he too had been at
everybody's beck and call, with no place in life to call
his own.

Well, it was too late to go into the church now. He
turned back the way he had come, to all the things that
would be waiting by now for him to do. But he did turn
aside for a few moments to see how one of the free
masons, whom he had come to know a little, was getting
on with the cushion-capitals that he was carving for the
pillars of the choir.

Standing beside the small bent craftsman, watching the
slow, sure work of the adze cutting out the deep chevron

pattern, he said, "Your new stirabout boy—Nick Redpoll, I heard someone call him—is he kin to any of the workmen?"

Serle, the Mason, watched the creamy stone flake away under the stroke of the adze. "Not kin to anyone that I know of," he said. "He just came hanging round the site like a stray dog, and the lads started giving him odd-jobs. He makes a good enough stirabout boy. Good with his hands, too, and seems interested in the building. Pity about that leg, he might have made a course-setter one day."

XII

NICK REDPOLL

It was a few weeks before Lovel found time to spare for wandering over to the building-site again. Next year the great roof beams would be going up, but now the choir was roofed with gray hurrying sky, and the soft wet wind from the west swooped in through the clerestory windows, plucking at the clothes of the men working up there on the scaffolding. The North Aisle was already covered in, not vaulted yet, but roofed with bare beams and rafters, and thick with warm shadows as you looked into it through the round-headed arches of the choir. Something moved in the shadows, and Lovel saw that it was the boy Nick. He was standing there, a coil of scaffolding rope over his free shoulder, propped on his crutch, his head tipped back to watch the men working on the roof of the South Aisle opposite. And there was a raw look of longing on his face that suddenly hurt Lovel deep inside himself.

It was only for a moment; and then Nick Redpoll looked around and saw him and grinned.

Lovel limped over to join him, and they stood together watching the men on the high hurdle-walk.

"Windy up there," Nick said after a little while.

"Windy," Lovel agreed.

"Soon be time to put her to bed for the winter."

Lovel glanced around quickly. That sounded like mason's jargon, but the boy would have picked up a good deal of that by now, anyway.

"Reckon Master Beornfred feels good every time he takes a look up there," Nick said. And after another companionable silence, "She's going to be a beauty!"

Still gazing up at the men on the scaffolding, Nick put out a hand and laid it on the shaft of the pillar beside him. And Lovel thought it was the way someone might lay his hand against a tree trunk, feeling the good soundness of the living timber. But almost in the same instant, he saw Nick's face freeze in horror, eyes wide and mouth open for a warning shout that would not come; and from overhead came a crash and a slithering sound and a cry; and his own gaze whipped back to the high spider-walk just as a plank came crashing down onto the floor of the choir.

There was a flurry of shouting. Somebody was clinging to the edge of the hurdle-walk, with his legs kicking convulsively in empty air; two of his mates were hauling him to safety. The captain of the team, standing below where the plank had narrowly missed him, was bellowing, "By the Horns of Saint Luke! Don't none of you know *yet* how to carry a plank in a breath of wind?"

A shuddering gasp beside him made Lovel look around again. Nick Redpoll had crumpled up at the base of the pillar, and was crouching there with one arm flung across his face.

Lovel stooped over him quickly; the tumult on the spider-walk could look after itself. "It's all right," he said. "It's all right. It was only the plank that came down."

Slowly, Nick Redpoll lowered his arm and looked up, past Lovel to the figures on the hurdle-walk, now arguing furiously and calling names. He tried to grin, but there was a queer pearly grayness about his face, and the freckles stood out black against it. He had the look of someone who has just had a nightmare and is not yet quite free of it.

"It was only the plank," Lovel said again.

"Aye. Just for the moment it looked like 'twas going to be Barty." Nick tried to make a joke out of it. "I must be gone in the cockloft, coming all over dithersome like that. They say the Devil looks after his own—and Barty couldn't fall off a spider-walk if he tried."

"No, it was you who did that, wasn't it?" Lovel heard his own voice before he knew that he had spoken.

"Did—what?" said Nick, playing for time.

"Fell off a spider-walk—and you did it again just now when you thought Barty was coming down. That was how you hurt your knee."

For a long moment, there was silence between them. On the hurdle-walk things had returned to normal. Then Nick turned his head stiffly. "Aye. More'n two year agone." He reached for his crutch. "I must be getting on, or they'll be howling for their rope over at the tower foot."

"Nick," Lovel said quickly, "after work stops this evening, come up to the hospital. If I'm not around, ask for me."

They stood looking at each other. Then Nick said, "And for why, Reverend Canon?"

"I would like to look at your knee."

"It mended stiff," Nick said, almost sullenly.

"Yes, I know. I'd like to look at it, all the same."

Nick looked down at his right hand, which had tightened into a fist. "Could you—G'arn, o'course you couldn't."

Lovel said, "I don't know whether I could or not. My grandmother had the Second Sight, but I haven't. Please Nick—after Vespers?"

"I'll be cooking for the lads."

"When you have finished cooking, then."

Nick went on staring at his fist. Then he nodded and turned away. "I'll come," he said over his shoulder, hitching up the coil of rope.

But Lovel was not sure he would; not quite sure, until late that evening Nick Redpoll was actually standing before him in the little crowded dispensary, looking as defiant as though he had been dragged there for a beating.

Lovel made him sit down on his own plank bed in the corner and strip off his tattered hose, then lit another candle and knelt down beside him. "Now, let me look."

But as usual it was not so much looking as feeling, and not so much feeling as looking with his hands. He could see the white puckered scar where an abscess had been, and feel the drawn tendon, tense and sharp like a bow-string at the back of Nick's leg, that had tightened and tightened, drawing the damaged knee up with it until it could not be straightened at all. When at last Lovel looked up, the boy's gaze, wide and blue and solemn, was waiting for him. Nick drew the tip of his tongue over his lower lip, but he didn't say anything.

"Does that hurt?" Lovel asked.

"Not now."

"It will, if I try to make it straight again."

"Do you—think you can?" Nick said hoarsely. "I'd like fine to get back to my trade."

Lovel got up, and went to see how the cough syrup that he was boiling over the brick stove in the corner was do-ing. Suddenly he was remembering across almost ten years, the time when he had had to decide much the same thing about Valiant. Nobody would hit Nick Redpoll on the head with a stone if he left that leg alone; he would just go on as he was. Mightn't that be better than hurting him as he would *have* to hurt him, and go on hurting him and making him hope, for months and months; and then, as like as not, have to admit defeat for both of them after all? But there was a chance. He had felt it with his hands on Nick's knee. *There was a chance.*

He turned around and looked at the stirabout boy across the candle flame. "I believe there is a chance," he said. "Go and pray to Saint Bartholomew; we could do with a good prayer. And I'll come and find you tomorrow."

Later still that evening, in the little wattle-and-daub cabin that was the Master's Lodging, Lovel stood before the table at which Rahere sat struggling with the everlasting hospital accounts. "We must go begging again," Rahere said. "But what we really need is another miracle. What would you be wanting, Brother Lovel?"

"I suppose a miracle too, Master," Lovel said.

Rahere smiled, and pushed the accounts on one side. "For miracles you should go across to our fine sky-roofed priory church. It should have stars between the clouds for altar candles, tonight. I haven't any miracles handy."

Lovel said, "There's this boy, Nick Redpoll—one of the stirabout boys over at the priory—"

"The boy with the crutch?"

"May I bring him into the hospital?"

"Is he sick?" asked Rahere.

"No. But I think it might be possible to get back the movement of his knee for him, if—if I could have him in here."

"For how long?"

"I don't know—maybe for half a year."

Rahere sighed and laid down the pen he had been playing with. The lines on his face looked in the candle-light deep and thin, as though they had been cut with a sword—both the lines of laughter and the lines of grief. "The building-site is not far off. Could you not do what-ever needs to be done if he came up here to you each day?"

"He would not come. The men would find work for him all the time, and—and he would not be in a fit state to do it, what's more. An old man-at-arms once told me that a hurt to the knee or elbow is the hardest of all to bear, and he will have a great deal of pain, and I can't do the work properly if he does not get the needful rest and tending with it."

"Nick Redpoll has been around the building-site for a month or more. Why this sudden interest?" Rahere said.

"I suppose I thought he was just another like me. It was only today I found out that it was only an accident—a fall from the scaffolding on another church. I have looked at his knee, and I am sure that something could be done." He looked at Rahere beseechingly. "It—it isn't only his leg, it's his whole life. He was learning the building trade —and if you saw the way he was watching the man on the hurdle-walk. . . . He has the right kind of hands, too, you can see it when he touches stone."

Rahere sat back, his winged eyebrows quirking. "Brother Lovel, I have never heard you in full spate before. So, if I let you have Nick Redpoll in here to mend him, you will give me another mason to build me my priory."

"Master, don't laugh at me," Lovel said, "other times,
but—not this time."

"Not this time, no," said Rahere. And indeed under the
flyaway brows, his face was very far from laughter. "So
then, you think there might be some hope of freeing the
boy's knee. But how much hope? Remember, we need
every bed. If we keep him here all winter, somebody will
die uncomforted in the gutter."

"He can have my bed in the dispensary."

"It is not only the bed, you know that. You know how
this hospital of ours is always ready to burst at the seams.
And how, if in the end 'I hope' proves to be only 'I want,
I desperately want'?"

Again Lovel remembered Valiant, and standing before
Brother Eustace in the infirmary at the New Minster. "I
do want," he began slowly. "It matters a great deal to
me—"

"I know it does," Rahere said, "and I know why."

"But I also believe that by God's Grace, there *is* hope—
I felt it, here in my hands."

Rahere was silent a long moment. Then he said, "So be
it, Brother Brat, and God's Grace and strength be with
you."

XIII

CARVED ANGELS

Nick's lodge was not best pleased at parting with him, for though, as he had said, they would soon be putting the priory church to bed for the winter, they would still be working on the site, cutting stone and shaping up timbers for next year; so they would still need a stirabout boy— and Nick was a good cook.

But it was all sorted out in the end by Michaelmas, an extra bed had been squeezed somehow into the long ward, close beside the dispensary door, and the long fight had begun.

For it was a fight, and Lovel and the redheaded boy fought it together through the weeks and months that followed. That autumn and winter Lovel worked on Nick's stiff knee with all the skill and caring and all the strength that was in him. He had had no training in what he was doing, because both Brother Eustace and Brother Peter would have left well—or ill—alone; and so he did not know with his head how to get the damaged joint moving again. He simply did what the queer knowledge in his hands told him needed doing.

To begin with he simply rubbed it every day with warm linseed oil and a decoction of scabius flowers which are good for loosening drawn tendons. That part was quite easy for both of them. It was later, when he began to feel the tight hardness of the tendon softening a little, that the bad time began. Then he really got to work, with fingers that seemed suddenly made of steel, pressing and probing and twisting, making Nick try to straighten his knee himself, again and again, harder and harder, until his face was white and spent and the sweat pricked out along the roots of his red hair. He went to Hal the blacksmith, too, and got him to make a kind of iron splint that bent in the middle but was just the smallest bit straighter than Nick's leg, and padded it with sheep's wool; and everyday when he had finished the rubbing and probing and pulling, he would bandage it on very tight, so that all the time it was pulling Nick's leg in the right direction.

Lovel knew how much that splint hurt, not only by the little gasp Nick sometimes gave when he was bandaging it on, but because in an odd way he could feel the pain through his hands into himself.

Once he said, "Nick, are you sorry we started this?"

And Nick shook his head, with his lower lip caught between his teeth. He couldn't speak just then.

But the day came when the splint did not hurt Nick

nearly as much, because his leg had straightened just enough to fit it. That was when Lovel knew that he was going to get Nick's leg straight again. But he would not know for a long time yet, whether it would ever bear his weight properly. So he only said, "Three days' rest, and then I'm taking this down to Hal to be straightened a bit more."

And so it went on.

Across the strip of rough ground, they had put the priory church to bed. But all day long the sounds of sawing and hammering and the clink of adze on stone came from the lodges, where the craftsmen were at their winter's work; and Master Beornfred came with his plans and drawings, and had long discussions with Rahere and Master Alfwine in the Master's Lodging.

And in the two long wards of the hospital, the sick-poor came and went, recovered or died. On Christmas Eve, with half a gale blowing from the northwest, and sleet spattering against the closed shutters, a beggar-woman's baby was born in the women's ward. Saint Bartholomew was the only hospital in London where a mother could go for care and shelter when her baby was born, and so there had been many babies born there by now, but never before, one on Christmas Eve. And Sister Ursula and Sister Maudlin, who had helped bring it into the world, were as happy about it as though they had just been in the stable at Bethlehem.

Lovel, making his late night rounds, was not so happy.

The mother was half-starved and the baby was too small, and when their time came to leave the hospital, there would be nothing for the woman to do but go back to begging again, for the baby now, as well as for herself. The fire on the central hearth between the two wards had sunk to a red glow that still gave off a wave of warmth as he paused beside it for a moment—the King gave them a tree-trunk every winter so that the hospital should not go cold—and the candle flames burned bright in the chapel, flaring a little in the drafts, their light coming and going on the picture of the saint and the scroll with the single butterfly perched on the edge of it. "The Lord shall comfort Zion. . . ." Lovel's gray depression lifted a little, because whatever happened to them afterward, there had been warmth and love and shelter for a little while, for the mother and the baby that had been born that night; and he felt less like shaking Sister Ursula and Sister Maudlin.

The candles burned all night, not only because of the chapel, but so that there should always be a little light in the wards; but it did not reach to the far end where Nick's bed was (nor did much of the warmth); but Lovel, pausing there before going through the dispensary door to his own bed, knew by his breathing that the boy was awake and in pain. It was only two days since the splint had been straightened again—for the fourth time.

"Not asleep?" Lovel whispered, above the snoring of the old man in the next bed.

"Never can sleep when the wind blows from this quarter," Nick said. He never admitted it when his leg was hurting. "Little 'un's in fine voice too, isn't he?"

For above the breathing and puffing and snoring of other sleepers, above the wing-beating of the wind and the sharp spatter of sleet, rose the thin fretful bleating of the new baby.

"He'll go to sleep soon," Lovel said. "He's finding the world something strange."

"Lor' bless you, I'm not complaining. Every hospital should have a new bratling on Christmas Eve," Nick said.

Next morning when Lovel arrived beside Nick's bed with the jar of rubbing oil, Nick, who usually spent most of his time lying on his back with his hands behind his head and staring up at the rafters, was sitting up and whittling away at a piece of wood, with a knife that didn't really look sharp enough for the job. The blanket was covered with chips and long curled shavings.

"I'm making a present for the baby," he explained rather shamefaced. "Maybe he won't cry so much if he has something to play with. Brother Luke found me the bit of wood."

"But not the knife," said Lovel.

"No. That was Sister Gertruda; it's not very sharp."

"Maybe she thought you were less likely to cut your thumb off with a blunt one. It's a mistake women make," Lovel said. "May I see?"

Nick put the small thing into the hand he held out. "It's a lamb," he said, in case there was any doubt.

But Lovel did not need to be told that. The little half-made figure was rough and clumsy, but there was no mistaking the shape, with its outsize unmanageable legs; and already Nick had managed somehow to catch the joyfulness of a very young lamb.

"It's not above half-finished yet," Nick said anxiously.

"I can see that. Have you often carved things?"

"Oh, I've whittled a bit from time to time—it's just a knack. Do you think the baby will like it, then?"

"I'm sure he will—when he's a little older." Lovel handed back the lamb, and began to roll up the sleeves of his habit. "If you'll wait a while, I'll find you a better knife, and that one can go back to the kitchen where it belongs."

Nick spent most of the rest of that day finishing the lamb; and that evening, Lovel took it down to the far end of the hospital-house, where the woman lay with her tiny wizened baby in the crook of her arm. "A boy in the other ward has made a gift for your baby," he said. "I should treasure it, if I were you."

The woman took the little lovingly carved lamb and looked at it, then she held it against her face and began to cry.

Lovel thought that he must give Nick something else to do, before he went back to staring at the rafters. But as it turned out, having once got started, Nick himself had the same thought, and next day, sitting on the edge of his bed—he was allowed up for a little while each day now—he said, "Brother Lovel, do you reckon you could get me a bit o' good carving wood—beech, say—out o' the carpenter's? 'Tisn't no good just lying here, and maybe I could make something for the chapel—for thank you, like."

Lovel stopped in his bandaging of the splint, and looked at him. "For thank you? We are going to get your leg straight Nick, but we have still to find how well it will take your weight, when we have done it."

Nick looked back at him steadily. "Aye, I know that. I'll make you an altar candlestick, all the same."

So Lovel got a piece of wood out of the carpenter's, and Nick set to work. Sister Aldis, who did most of the ward sweeping complained a good deal at first about shavings on the floor; but after Nick showed her what he was making, she admitted, rather grudingly, that it was worth a little extra sweeping. For Nick's candlestick was going to be no ordinary candlestick, but a tall long-winged angel with a crown on his head, and the candle-socket rising from between his back-folded wings.

It was by far the most difficult thing that he had ever tried to carve, and he didn't know how to do it; so he felt his way along slowly, doing what the wood seemed to want him to do, much as Lovel was doing with his stiff knee. He made mistakes; he could not get the hands as he wanted them; and the two sides of the angel's face came out not quite the same as each other, and he wasn't at all satisfied with it himself. But all the same, as the days went by, and the carved angel got nearer and nearer to being finished, Lovel knew that it was beautiful.

"I'll make another after this," Nick said. "There should be the pair—an' I'll know what not to do next time."

Lovel sat turning the figure over and over in his hands and looking at it. "You know," he said, "you could make your living as an image maker."

"You mean—if I can't be a mason."

Lovel looked up quickly. He had never pretended with Nick. "Yes," he said.

Nick looked at the carved angel as though he were seeing it for the first time, and was surprised at what he saw. "It's a thought," he said slowly. "Aye, it's a thought. . . ."

"You don't sound as though it was a thought you like very much."

" 'Twouldn't be the same, you see," Nick frowned, trying to explain what he meant. "It's so small, and—oh it's fine to do in between whiles, but it's not like the other —the walls going up, and the stones shaped true so's you can't scarce run your thumbnail along the joints, and knowing 'tis strong and sound and won't never fall down because all the weight comes in the right places and the buttresses are taking the strain fair and square and nothing out of kilter. And yet all seems like 'twas reaching up to the sky instead of crushing down on the earth—"

He broke off, suddenly flushing scarlet. "Here—give it me back, I haven't finished the crown yet."

He was sitting on the edge of his bed with his splinted leg stuck awkwardly out in front of him because it was nearly straight now. Lovel said, "If you start on that second angel tomorrow, we might try your weight on your knee about the time it's finished."

The year had turned, and the evenings were beginning to draw out, when at last the day came. Nick had saved the final polishing of his second angel to do that morning, as though finishing the angel and testing out his knee had become somehow, two things that belonged together. But it was finished and standing with the other before the saint's picture, carrying its burden of light, when Lovel came with the rubbing oil and his sleeves rolled up. It was just after the midday meal, and Nick's platter was still on the bed beside him, full of a cold stewed mess of some kind that he had hardly touched. "Not hungry," he said when Lovel asked him, and wrinkled his nose at the platter. Certainly the bean stew did look even more unappetizing than usual, but Lovel had a feeling that that was only an excuse. . . .

He set to work with the rubbing oil as usual, but when he had finished, instead of bandaging the splint on again, he gave Nick his crutch and helped him up. "Get the feel of it first—you'll miss the splint."

Nick stood and looked at him for a moment, the

freckles standing out very black across the bridge of his nose. And Lovel saw the appeal in his face and understood it. Not with Sister Ursula who was clearing up after the meal, not with Brother Philip, and the folk in the other beds, all looking on.

It was one of those days that come in late winter, suddenly soft and milky with promise, though there might be blizzards still to come. In the physic garden on the south side of the hospital it would be warm as spring. Nick would come to no harm out there.

"Come outside," he said.

There was a side door from the dispensary into the physic garden. Lovel led the way, hearing the tap of Nick's crutch behind him. There were blue-green snowdrop spears clustered about the doorsill, and a blackbird was singing in the nearest elder tree. A straight turf path led from the door straight across the garden, between the still bare beds where garlic and celandine, foxglove and feverfew and elecampane would soon be showing green again; and where it started, they stood for a moment looking at each other. "Are you ready?" Lovel said.

Nick said nothing, but nodded.

And Lovel took his crutch and moved backward a step. "Now—walk toward me—no, look at me, not at your feet."

For a long moment Nick did not move. His eyes were fixed on Lovel's face. Lovel moved backward another step.

He was suddenly remembering Valiant again, and the stable at the New Minster. His throat ached with anxiety. "Come," he said.

Nick, with enormous care and concentration, took a step, and then another, and another—five steps, and then Lovel caught him as he stumbled, and gave him back his crutch.

He was grinning from ear to ear, and shivering. "I did it! I did it!"

"Don't crow!" Lovel said. "And next time, remember to bend your knee. God gave you that knee for bending, and you're carrying it as stiff as a broomstick! Now come indoors."

In the dispensary, Nick hung back from the doorway to the ward. "When can I go back to the building?"

"To being a stirabout boy?"

"There's many a good free mason started that way."

Lovel nodded. "Not for a while yet. Five steps does not mean you are back on your feet, and I have to make sure it won't start tightening up again, before I let you go." He smiled. "You had better start carving something else."

Nick was silent a moment, and then the corners of his mouth curled slowly upward. "Not I! I know something this place wants more than an image maker."

"And what would that be?"

"A cook!" said Nick.

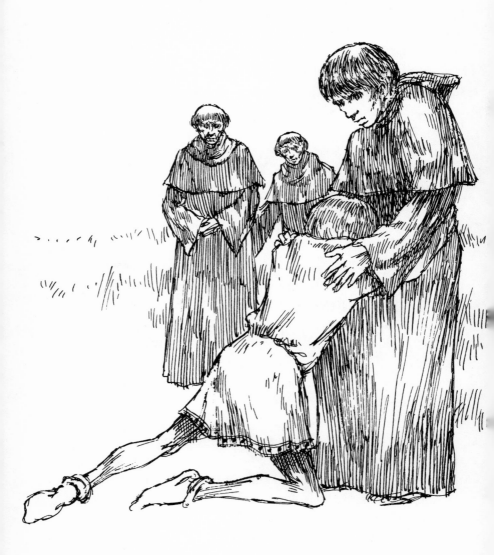

XIV

THE MIRACLE

A few days later, Lovel went across to the priory in search of Serle. The masons had set up their winter workshop under cover of the roofed-in North Aisle, and there he found the man he was looking for among cut stone and column heads, chipping away at a string course. It had been an open winter, and so they had been able to get a fair amount of work done, ready for when building started again, around Eastertime.

When they had exchanged good-days, Lovel came straight to the point. "You remember Nick Redpoll?"

Serle looked up from his work. "Aye, I mind Nick Redpoll. How does the lad?"

"He can walk a fair bit without his crutch, now," Lovel said. "By the time you start building again, he'll be fit for work."

"Always room for a good stirabout boy. We've missed his cooking."

Lovel sighed. "We shall miss it, too. He's been working in the hospital kitchen while his leg finishes mending. But it is not his cooking that I came to talk to you about. You said last autumn that he might have made a course-setter."

"Aye, but for the leg." Serle made a careful cut with his adze.

"But with a sound leg?"

"Sound enough for work on the high catwalks?"

"He may always have a slight limp; but sound enough for the high catwalks, yes."

"Then—aye, he might make a course-setter."

"That's just it. He was learning that trade before the accident to his knee; but I think, given the chance, he'd make not just a course-setter but a free mason."

Serle stopped work altogether and stood up, rubbing his chin with a rasping sound. "Do you now, Canon Lovel. And what makes you think that?" He grinned. "Every man to his own trade, they do say, and—asking your pardon—I never heard tell that yours was handling stone."

Lovel began carefully to unroll something that he had brought with him wrapped in a bit of sackcloth. "Look at this," he said, and set the second of Nick Redpoll's long-winged angels on the flat top of the stone block that Serle had been working.

Serle picked it up and looked at it, with eyebrows

raised and mouth puckered as though in a soundless
whistle. "Nick made this? I mind he used to whittle
a bit."

"Yes," Lovel said.

"It's pretty. Aye, it's good work, for a youngling. But
a little wooden angel don't make a free mason. Stone's
different from wood; and all this—" he jerked a thumb
over his shoulder in a gesture that took in the still roofless
choir, the piled ashlars in the aisle and all the great
church that would stand there one day but was as yet
only a few foundations and a stack of drawings in the
Master Mason's tracing-shed—"all this is different from
a little figure you can pick up in one hand. . . . You
know what—the lad could do well as an image maker."

Lovel smiled. "I told him that. He said it wasn't the
same—not the same as walls going up and the stones
shaped true, so that you couldn't run your thumbnail
along the joints, and knowing it would never fall down
because all the weight and stresses came in the right places
and nothing was out of kilter (whatever that means) and
—and yet seeming all the time to be reaching up to the
sky instead of crushing down on the earth."

There was a small silence filled with the sounds of
the other masons at work. "He said that, did he," Serle
said at last.

"So nearly as I can remember. So I brought you the
angel to show you that he *has* craft-skill in his hands."

"Craft-skill small isn't the same as craft-skill big."

"Surely not, but I thought that the ability to carve detail was one of the skills needful in a free mason." Lovel looked at the fine chevron pattern of the string-course that Serle had been at work on.

"One of them, aye. But even at that, it's like I said, wood's not stone—the lad understands wood, I grant you."

"And if he understands wood—and if he feels as he does about all this—" Lovel glanced about him at the same things that Serle had indicated with his thumb— "mightn't it at least be worth finding out whether he can understand stone?"

"Aye," Serle said at last. "But you'd best be saying your piece to the Master Mason. It's not me that does the hiring in these parts."

"I have already spoken with Master Beornfred. He'll try Nick as a course-setter and let him work his way from there, if he can."

"Well then, what would you be wanting me to do about it?" Serle was surprised and a little put out.

"Keep a kindly eye on him. Try him at the job—and if you find him worth it, let him learn from your skill."

Serle was silent a moment, looking at the carved angel in his hands. Then abruptly he nodded, and handed it back. "I'll do that. But no more, mind. Nothing but his own skill can make him a free mason."

At Easter the priory church woke from its winter sleep, and Nick Redpoll, with nothing left of the old injury but a limp that showed when he was tired, went back to work on the site, but no longer as a stirabout boy. Lovel did not even see him go, for it was the day of the weekly horse-market, and a man who had been kicked by a frightened colt was brought in just as Nick was gathering up his few belongings; and by the time the fellow's broken head was sewn up, there was nothing left of Nick Redpoll but his empty bed in the corner, and the pair of long-winged angels who now held the altar candles in the little chapel.

And from the Master to the newest patient who had been there long enough to remember it, Saint Bartholomew's Hospital sighed and resigned itself to Sister Gertruda's cooking again.

Spring turned to summer, and the life of the hospital went on as usual. Folk came and went, got better or died; the herbs in the physic garden flourished; and Rahere said Mass everyday in the altar chapel where the two wards met, and went on struggling with the accounts and the complaints and all the problems that the master of a busy hospital had to deal with.

And across the strip of rough ground that divided hospital from priory, the great roof beams of the choir were hoisted into place, and the tower began to rise.

Summer drew on, and the great three-day cloth-fair came and went. The choir was roofed in now, and the archway beyond which the nave of the church would one day rise, had been roughly boarded up, so that it made a complete building in which services could be held. And the day came, on the very edge of autumn, when the Bishop of London—that same Richard de Belmain who had received Lovel's vows four years ago—was to consecrate the priory church of Saint Bartholomew.

It was a gray stormy day of low drifting cloud with the smell of rain in the wind. But the rain was still holding off when the Bishop's procession followed by Rahere and his black-gowned canons, and the master craftsmen in their Sunday best, wound its way in through the small doorway that had been left in the boarded-up west end of the choir. Inside it was very dark, a great shell of empty shadow, with the gray clouds hurrying past the high clerestory windows that had no glass in them as yet. And in all the grayness, the scarlet and crimson and purple of the Bishop and his clergy glowed jewel-deep in the glimmer of the candles on the makeshift altar. The scent of incense drifted on the air, and the chanting voices of the Brothers rose and hung high under the shadowy roof. Lovel thought how soon nave and tower and transcept would rise about them, and the buildings of the great priory itself; and it all seemed a great way from the long low-roofed hospital house close by, where his sick folk waited for him to come back to them. Two separate worlds. He looked at the tall black cranefly figure of Rahere who had been the King's Jongleur and then the master of the hospital and would be Prior here by and by, and wondered if it seemed as strange and remote to him. But Rahere's face in the light of the altar candles was as hard to read as the face of a Crusader knight on a tomb.

Lovel pulled his thoughts back to his devotions.

The Bishop's hand was raised in blessing; his strong rather harsh voice filled the tall building. "This spiritual house, Almighty God shall inhabit, and bless and glorify it. His seeing and His hearing shall be toward it night and day, that the asker in it shall receive, the seeker shall find, and he who knocks shall enter in. . . ."

The sun that had been hidden all day broke through the clouds, and the clerestory windows were suddenly full of light; great shafts of light that shone down into the heart of the choir, filling all the building with a sudden radiance that dimmed the altar candles.

Lovel thought, "The asker shall receive, the seeker shall find, and he who knocks shall enter in—joy and gladness shall be found therein, thanksgiving and the voice of melody—not two worlds but one." He saw Rahere's strange haunted face fly open into joy.

Outside, the work had stood still for an hour, that the ceremony might not be marred by hammering and sawing; but as everyone came out into the still lingering sunshine, it was beginning again. The first tier of scaffolding was up around the tower, which now stood close on fifteen feet high, and already there were workmen up there. The head of one of them shone red as flame in the sunlight.

As soon as the procession had broken up, Lovel came back. He had only a few moments to spare; there was work waiting for him, but he came back, and found Nick Redpoll climbing down the ladder to meet him. It was as though they had arranged to meet; and yet they didn't seem at first to have anything special to say.

"How is the knee?" Lovel asked.

"It aches a bit by the end of the day, but it's getting better all the time."

They stood looking up at the choir and the part-built tower rising proud against the stormy sky, with the craftsmen and laborers swarming around it.

"There were times, you know," Lovel said, still watching the men on the hurdle-walk, "when I wondered if you could take very much more. When you are a master mason like Master Beornfred, you'll be able to feel that maybe you've earned it more than most."

There was a small silence, and then Nick Redpoll turned to look down at Lovel. He had grown a lot during his time in the hospital, and could look down quite a long way. He swallowed, and suddenly flushed fiery pink to the roots of his hair. "Well it's like this. If it'd been Brother Dominic or even Brother Luke, I reckon I couldn't have took it; but 'twas you, you see."

"And so?" said Lovel.

Nick swallowed again. "Well you see, 'twasn't so lonely that way—like having a mate with you in a tight place. When the pain was bad and that, I says to myself, 'It's

Brother Lovel, with a game leg of his own, and that humpy shoulder and all, and *he knows*,' and so I hangs on."

"I see," Lovel said after a moment. "Yes I do see, I—thank you, Nick."

And then, just as it had happened the first time they met, someone up on the hurdle-walk was roaring for Nick Redpoll, and he had to go.

Lovel stood where he was, still staring at the growing stump of the church tower. He felt suddenly very tired. He was generally tired, but it was only sometimes that he noticed it. He must, by Brother Eustace's reckoning, have bled quite a lot of his own life away with Nick Redpoll. And with the sudden tiredness came a wonderful quiet, and in the midst of the quiet, a sense of freedom—freedom from all the things that were tangled up with having been stoned out of his village for being a witch's brat. And yet he knew that in another way he would never be free again, because he would belong to every sick soul who came into his care.

A hover of butterflies, brought out by the sudden warmth, danced across the raw new stoneface of the tower; and again a memory brushed across Lovel's mind, hesitated on the edge of being lost, and then stayed. "You will be one of the menders of this world; not the makers, nor yet the breakers; just one of the menders. . . . When the time comes, you'll know."

Nick had reached the top of the ladder.

"That was a good miracle," said Rahere's voice behind him.

"A good miracle," Lovel agreed.

Both Lovel and Nick Redpoll would have been surprised if they had known that in later years, among the list of miracles credited to Saint Bartholomew's Priory was that of a boy called Nicholas who had been instantly healed there of a stiff leg, and in gratitude had stayed on to work in the kitchens.

Rosemary Sutcliff was born in southern England and has lived there almost all her life. She was very ill as a small child and had to spend several years in bed, when her mother read to her a great deal. She was enjoying books by Dickens, Thackeray and Trollope from the age of five onward, and she developed an intense interest in history and historical stories while she was still very young. Rosemary Sutcliff left school at fourteen to attend Bideford Art School, where she specialized in miniature painting. She was elected a member of the Royal Society of Miniature Painters just after the Second World War.

In 1950 Rosemary Sutcliff's first book for children appeared, and since then she has written many historical stories for young people, as well as some adult novels, establishing herself as one of the leading British writers of historical fiction. *The Lantern Bearers* was awarded the British Library Association's Carnegie Medal for 1959 as the outstanding book for children published during that year.